Joseph Paul Haines

Ten With a Flag

and other playthings

Stories

GryffynPerch Books

GryffynPerch Books
Aurora, CO 80011

PRAISE FOR THE STORIES OF JOSEPH PAUL HAINES

"Haines takes some of the harsh realities of life, like alcoholism, cancer, and child abuse, and juxtaposes them with the magic of childhood, Oz, and the Emerald City to create a story with substance and its own unique charm." -- Nicole McClain, Tangent Magazine

"Similarly creepy, and similarly memorable is another story of parenting gone wrong: Copper Angels by Joseph Paul Haines . . ." -- Bluejack, The Internet Review of Science Fiction

"The Man Behind the Curtain" by Joseph Paul Haines is moving and emotionally believable . . ." -- Rich Horton, SF Reviews

"The tale itself is a wonderful construct: oppressive governments, human beings given a rating which then in turn influences how they exist in the social infrastructure – all these are terrifying and yet compelling concepts of the future. . . It's a catch 22; a moral dilemma for a short, satirical anecdote that I found the most enjoyable of all this collection."--Matthew Tate, Horrorscope Magazine

"All in all, it's an excellent story, and one that adds the name of Joseph Paul Haines to the rapidly growing list of authors I'll be keeping an eye out for in the future. "-- Paul J. Iutzu, Tangent Magazine

"February's winning story is Scratch, written by Joseph Paul Haines. It combines great dialog, a great idea and one of the most stomach turning paragraphs I have ever had the pleasure to read!"--Andrew Hannon, Editor of Thirteen Magazine.

For all the women in my life who've given me hope, courage and the strength to keep fighting, this is for Susan, Kathy, Dee, Katherine, Angela, but most of all this is for my beautiful wife Catherine, without whom none of this would even matter. You will always be my butterfly princess.

CONTENTS

INTRODUCTION

by

Samantha Henderson

It's the voices that get to you. That haunt you, that crawl under your skin, that whisper in your ear in those few fuzzy seconds before sleeping and waking.

The terrible innocence of a child who only wants to protect her baby brother. The terror of a corrupt detective encountering an eldritch horror. The mute patience of a dog, following his master into an in-between fantasy world that destroys the canine loyal. A woman who must choose between her husband or the state controlling her destiny, with a price to be paid either way. A man in search of his sister and the magic that might save him. A high school football hero down on his luck, flipping through the could-have-beens of a life that might or might not be well lived. Their voices chatter under the skin, like the itch inflicted on the protagonist of "Scratch."

The fiction of Joseph Paul Haines explores and exposes the voices of people who sin dreadfully, against themselves and against others, and yet their motivations resonate and it's difficult to condemn them. These stories are science fiction, fantasy, magic realism. But they are unified in this – there's a darkness to them. Sometimes it's like a pleasant swirl of bittersweet chocolate, sometimes the acrid tang of black coffee you drink to keep awake on a 24-hour drive.

Full disclosure: I was in an online writer's group with Joseph, my first. In some ways your first critique group is like your first lover – they mark you, for good or ill. We took turns posting stories, and whenever one of Joe's came on board, I always felt a delicious anticipation: what has he done now? Will the chocolate be bitter or sweet? Sometimes it was one, sometimes the other – but never disappointing.

My advice to you – read these stories slowly, like an expensive treat. They are all, in their own way, delicious. But I've warned you, and I'm not responsible for how long the voices will linger in your head.

Samantha Henderson's short stories and poetry have appeared in Realms of Fantasy, Strange Horizons, Clarksworld, Weird Tales, Chizine, Fantasy, Lone Star Stories, Abyss and Apex, Goblin Fruit, Mythic Delirium and Stone Telling, as well as the anthologies Running with the Pack, Steampunk Reloaded and the upcoming Lace and Blade III. Her dark Victorian fantasy Heaven's Bones was released in 2008, and together with Kendall Evans she is the winner of the 2010 Rhysling Award in the long-form category for their poem, "On the Astronaut Asylum." "Bottles," the film based on her short story of the same name, was the winner of Best Fantasy Short and Best Screenplay at the 2010 DragonCon Independent Film Festival. She lives in Covina with her family and various other creatures.

Ten with a Flag

Johnnie didn't talk while he was driving. Normally it would drive me a little crazy, sitting there in traffic and not saying a word, but this time it didn't bother me. There was too much on my mind. Truth was, I hoped he wouldn't talk so that I could have some time to think. But when he pulled onto the freeway, I knew I wasn't going to get that lucky.

It only took him a couple of seconds to connect to the traffic web. Johnnie didn't like being out of control, it was one of the things I'd found endearing in him; quaint even. This time though, he didn't even double-check the connection. The steering wheel folded and collapsed into the dash, and he turned to face me. "What does that mean, exactly?" he asked. "Did the doctor say anything else?"

I shook my head. "He said he'd have to check, but he'd never heard of the combination coming up before."

"He'd have to check?"

"Yeah."

"Did he say anything else?"

"I told you, he said he'd have to check." I didn't know what to say. It was still sinking in.

Johnnie leaned back in his seat and stared out his window. I could tell he was getting ready to turn around and go back. We'd only been married three years, but I could read some of his expressions like a book. "How's that even possible?" he asked. "I mean, is the baby okay?"

"The baby is fine."

"Now I wish we didn't know."

I turned away from him. "You agreed we should get the test done."

"I know, but . . .*damn*."

"Don't you think it's better knowing?"

"How do you get a ten and a flag?" he asked.

"He said he'd have to check," I repeated.

"But the baby's fine?"

"Yes."

"Are you sure he said ten?"

I nodded. "Ten."

Johnnie crossed his arms and chewed on his bottom lip. I think he mumbled something, but at that point I didn't want to hear it.

We didn't talk for a while after that. I was contented to sit and watch the other transports as we cut in and out of traffic. It was like watching a school of fish swimming together, weaving at the same time. We rushed along at speeds of over two hundred kilometers with no more than a meter separating our vehicles, our safety in the control of the central traffic computer. Sometimes it was easier to let something bigger than yourself take control. It had a plan, and although you couldn't always see it, you knew you'd never wreck.

It wasn't until we sped past our off-ramp that I began to get concerned.

"Where we going?" I asked.

Johnnie didn't answer. He punched up the navigation screen and sighed. "What the hell?"

"What?"

"We've been redirected. We have an appointment with Human Services. Now."

"Now?"

"Yeah, they've even rescheduled my work-shift for this afternoon and notified the office."

"Do you think it's about the test results?" I had expected some reaction from Human Services, just not this quick. I folded my hands in my lap to keep from tapping my fingers. Johnnie didn't like to see me get nervous.

"It doesn't say."

"Great." There was nothing else to do but sit back and enjoy the ride. We were just passengers.

Central had control.

"I understand you must be apprehensive," the agent said. He was a small man, this Mr. White, and the huge, empty desk he sat behind made him look even smaller.   "Results like these can cause a great deal of confusion."

Johnnie started to say something. I squeezed his hand before he could. The last thing we needed was to anger a government official, particularly one as high up as Mr. White seemed to be. It was best to remain compliant until he finished.

"The important thing to remember is that your baby rated a ten. Your child will be an asset to the Nation. Only one in fifty thousand couples that go through the procedure come up with these results. It's a credit to the two of you as citizens.

"As such, the state has raised both your rating to eight, effective immediately. Congratulations."

Johnnie and I stared at each other. Eights? That was two levels higher than our current rating.   Eight meant ten hours of work as opposed to forty. Eight meant no more scraping by between allowance periods. Eight meant a much bigger apartment. Eight meant no more late nights while Johnnie stayed at work to improve his production numbers.

Eight meant no more looking over our shoulders.

"Thank you, Mr. White." But of course, Johnnie couldn't keep his mouth shut. "I've just one question, though. The flag? How can there be a flag with a rating of ten?"

Mr. White pursed his lips. It was quite an odd gesture, almost feminine and I had to keep myself from giggling.

Eight didn't mean you could just randomly disrespect government officials.

"Well," he said, "there is that question.   To be perfectly honest, I've never seen it come up before. But in your case, I don't think it's something to worry about. Your child rated a ten and you are now eights. I don't see how there could be a problem. The government won't, of course, stand in the way if you decide to invoke your option."

"What if we do?" Johnnie asked.   I squeezed his hand tighter but he just pulled his away from my grasp and continued, "What would happen to us?"

Mr. White smiled. There was little humor in it. "Happen, sir?"

"If we use the option to terminate the pregnancy, what would happen to us?"

"Why would you do that, sir? Your child is a ten. He or she will be a great credit to the nation and improve life for all of the citizenry. What citizen would even consider that?"

Johnnie shook his head. "Well, the flag. I'm worried about it."

"Worried about it?" Mr. White picked up his pen and scribbled something on his tablet.

"Yes," Johnnie answered.

"Your child is a ten, sir," Mr. White repeated. "That should be enough to make you forget about the flag."

"Well, it doesn't. It certainly didn't keep Central from issuing the flag. Why would they have issued a flag unless there was some concern?"

Mr. White tapped his pen on his desk a few times, and leaned forward. "How much do you know about the CDP test?"

"Central looks into the future and determines the baby's community viability," Johnnie said. "That's really all there is to it, right?"

Mr. White chuckled. "Well, that's not really accurate. Central can't look into the future. That's impossible," he said, chuckling. "What it does do is predict the future based off of the child's cellular past, the parent's cellular past and other environmental factors. You see, once you can witness the cellular history of an individual, you can predict future activity through sheer computational power. Central has an over ninety-nine percent success rate with this test. We don't question the results."

I knew Johnnie wasn't going to take the hint so I cut him off before he could do more damage. "It's just so confusing, Mr. White," I said, smiling as wide as I could. "Aren't flags usually reserved for children with . . . well, problems?"

"Actually," he said, "the flag is just an indication that the parents will have to make a sacrifice. Sometimes it means that the child will be handicapped, and the parents will have to work additional hours to make up for the extra burden on the State. All we know is that when a flag comes up, the sacrifice necessary from the parents is sufficient to warrant giving them the option to terminate the pregnancy. It's how we protect your freedoms as individuals.

"The State values that highly." He smiled.

"But our child is a ten," I said. "Tens can't be a burden on the State by definition. They are the ones that make the State better."

"That's true. Which is why I'm not overly concerned with the flag. And neither should you. Your child will be an asset to the State. You'll have to make a sacrifice, but what parent doesn't?"

I knew I had to phrase my next question carefully. "And there's no indication as to what form that sacrifice might take?"

"You know I can't answer that," Mr. White said. "And you know you shouldn't even be asking. Knowledge of the results can affect their outcome."

"I see. Well, thank you--"

"You didn't answer my question," Johnnie said. "What happens if we take the flag option?"

Mr. White fidgeted in his chair. "Well, your promotion will be cancelled, for one thing." He grabbed a folder from the stack of papers and flipped it open. "You're a six now, correct?"

Johnnie nodded.

"Hmm," Mr. White said, flipping through pages. "Did you know that your boss had put in for a rate reduction?"

"Excuse me?" Johnnie leaned forward in his seat. I could see his cheeks turning red. "I work harder than--"

"Says here," Mr. White interjected, "that your boss seems to think that although you spend fifty hours a week on the job, your production levels only account for thirty hours worth of work. He recommended you be downgraded to a five so that you can actually accomplish forty hours worth of work in sixty hours time."

"That's not right. I work harder than--"

"But you don't have to worry about that anymore," Mr. White said, smiling wider. "You've been promoted to an eight."

Johnnie's mouth hung open. It was time to get out of there. "Thank you, Mr. White. We both appreciate your time."

Johnnie was still dazed by the time we got back to the transport. It didn't help matters any that it wasn't the same one we had left in the parking garage. It was bigger. Longer. It was a transport belonging to a couple of eights. There was no driver's seat.

Central had control.

"A demotion?" Johnnie said. "I can't believe that--"

"No," I said, nodding toward the speaker panel on the dashboard. "A promotion. What great luck." Doubt gnawed at my insides, but this wasn't the place to discuss it.

We sat quietly while Central directed the car onto the freeway. Once again, we passed our off-ramp without slowing.

"Central," Johnnie said. "List destination."

The soft voice of Central command filled the cabin, "Your new residence, sir."

"New residence, of course."

"You have eighteen voice messages, sir, all offering congratulations on your promotion and the impending boon to the Nation that your son's birth will deliver. Would you like to hear them?"

So it was a boy.

Neither of us felt much like celebrating. "Not now, Central," I said. "Just take us home."

We'd managed to go a full week without appearing in public. The raise meant Johnnie could work from home, so we didn't have to go out if we didn't want but we both knew we'd stayed hidden as long as we could. I'd convinced Johnnie to show our faces at the opera--I'd never been to the opera; it was one of the perks of the promotion and I was looking forward to the evening--but even that had been a struggle. Since we'd come home from Human Services, he'd spent all his free time in front of the computer. He wouldn't even discuss the test results with me.

My wardrobe had picked out a deep-blue chiffon evening gown for me. I dressed in front of the full-length mirror and once I was ready, the lights dimmed while the environmental controls chose the scent of roses to fill the room. It was the first time in weeks I'd felt relaxed. A night out would do us good. I only hoped Johnnie would be in a similar mood.

Instead, I found Johnnie still sitting in front of the computer. He hadn't yet started to get ready. "We'll be late," I said.

He glanced my direction and did a double take. "You look beautiful."

I crossed one ankle over the other, dipped my chin and looked up at him. "Then get up, get dressed and take me on a date."

He sighed, took a deep breath and said, "I *do* so very love you, you know."

"Then get dressed."

He pushed himself away from the desk and walked toward his dressing room.

"And don't even try," I called after him, "to pick something out yourself. Just wear what your wardrobe chooses. You'd never match this color if you had all night."

"I'm not completely useless."

"Oh honey, I know that," I said, smiling as sweetly as possible. "You're only useless when trying to dress yourself. Now hurry up!"

We made it out the door on time.

Our new transport was nowhere to be seen. An older model pulled up in front of our building.

"I requested a downgrade for the evening," Johnnie said. "I felt like driving."

I shook my head. "As long as you get us there on time."

He held my door open and closed it behind me. I waited until we left the parking lot and slid my hand onto his leg. It was good to be out again. Even though the new apartment had plenty of room, it just felt great to get out from behind the walls, to get back into the world again.

Once we'd turned onto the surface streets, Johnnie engaged the auto-drive and leaned back in his seat. "I thought you said you wanted to drive?"

"I lied. I just wanted to talk to you without a speaker."

My good mood evaporated. "Do we have to do this now?"

"Did you know," he asked without acknowledging my question, "that in the four cases where a mother has died in childbirth over the last ten years, the flag option had been available in every case?"

My stomach turned. "So? That doesn't mean--"

"No, no, it doesn't mean--"

"So why are you bringing this up?" I asked. "Don't you think I'm frightened enough already?"

Johnnie leaned closer to me. "But it doesn't mean it isn't possible, either. We've got to consider it."

"It could also mean that our son will have a learning disability, and we'll have to work particularly hard to get him through it." My cheeks were burning. I understood his concern, but I couldn't believe he was going to ruin our first night out together in ages.

He crossed his arms. "And it could mean you're in danger. How are we supposed to know? Who's to say the child actually needs us to be a ten?"

"We can't know. Knowledge of future events can change the outcome. He's a ten. That's all that's important."

"Bullshit."

My jaw dropped.

"That's not *all* that's important by a long-shot."

"Of course it is." Instinct made me look around to see that no one was in the car with us. "You don't interfere with something like that. It's almost treasonous."

"Of course it isn't treasonous. The State wouldn't have given us the flag otherwise. It's our right."

My eyes filled with tears. "But he's going to be a ten. He's going to be a perfect little boy."

"Yes, he will," Johnnie replied, taking my hand in his. He brushed a tear from my cheek and added, "But perfect for who?"

I knew we weren't going to the opera even before we sped past the turn-off to the Cultural District, but it didn't get any easier once we were sitting inside Dr. Jones' office, waiting for him to finish his examination. "Well," he said, looking down at me from over the edge of his bifocals, "there's no genetic contra indicators, no signs of pre-toxemia, no anemia, nothing that would give me even a moment's hesitation about your health or that of your child." He seemed tired and his thin, grey hair puffed up more on one side of his head than the other.

Johnnie ran his fingers through his hair. "I just don't get it."

"Maybe it's not for us to get," I offered. "But there's nothing wrong with me. I'm not in any danger so we can stop worrying--"

"That doesn't mean that something couldn't show up later though, right?"

"Johnnie, I--"

"Nothing is certain, sir," Dr. Jones replied.

"Johnnie!" I grabbed his wrist and clamped down. He whipped his head around to look at me, and that's when I finally saw it: He was terrified. Sweat beaded his upper lip and he couldn't keep his eyes on any one thing.

"But it's still your choice," Dr. Jones said. "No one is going to stop you from choosing to exercise your option. The flag is there for a purpose."

I stared Johnnie in the eye, hoping he'd notice the slight side-to-side shake I was giving him.

"I think we should use the flag," he said.

My skin froze. "No," I whispered.

"There will be other babies," he said. "Ones without a flag. We don't need the raises. I can't stand the thought of losing you. Tell her she can have other babies, Doctor."

"Of course you can have other babies," Dr. Jones said, "but let's not overlook--"

"Why should we have to make a sacrifice?" Johnnie asked, kneeling down in front of me. "We've been given the option. There wouldn't be a flag if there weren't a problem. You know that."

I tried to speak, but nothing came out of my mouth. He was right. There was something wrong; some kind of difficulty we'd have to face if we had this baby. Difficulties we most likely wouldn't have to face with another baby. But this one was a ten! He could be a great composer or an artist. He could discover medicine that cured the last remaining diseases. He could do anything! I *knew* that, felt it with every beat of my heart.

The State knew that too.

But what was the cost?

I looked at Johnnie and felt very cold.

"I can't make this decision," I said. I pulled him in close and rested my cheek against his and whispered in his ear. "You make it. Make it for both of us."

He kissed my temple, then my cheek, then my ear. His warm breath caught in his throat. He pulled away, turned to Dr. Jones and said, "We'll take the option."

What little air remained in my chest rushed out of me. The room spun.

"Very well," Dr. Jones said. He removed a gown from a drawer beneath the examination table and handed it me. "I'll give you a moment to get ready," he said, and left the room.

We didn't talk. I changed into the dressing gown and sat back up on the table. The longer we sat, waiting, the smaller the room seemed to get. I wanted Johnnie to say something; anything, but he just sat there, trying his best to smile when I looked at him.

After a few minutes, Dr. Jones re-joined us. He wasn't alone.

Mr. White from Human Services stood in the doorway, flanked by a half dozen Constables. "That will be all, Doctor."

Johnnie stepped in front of me. "What are you doing? This is our decision."

"And you made it," Mr. White said. He appeared even smaller out from behind his desk.

Johnnie shook his head and held his arms to the side, trying in vain to shield me from the Constables. "You said you wouldn't interfere."

Mr. White smiled. "We didn't. We allowed you to make your decision of your own free will." He stepped inside the door and removed a stun gun from behind his back. "No one ever said we'd let you go through with it, though. The flag is an option, not a right. Arrest him."

The Constables fell on him then. Johnnie tried to resist, but one kick in the stomach was all it took to end that. Within ten seconds they had him out of the room, leaving only Mr. White and myself. "Go ahead and get changed," he said. "I'll wait for you outside."

I dressed slowly. It was as if every memory I had of Johnnie came back to me right then. The dates, our wedding, the fights, the make-ups; all of it. I'd just stood there and let them take him. I wanted to cry, but held it back. Whatever happened to us, I'd be strong. I pulled my shoulders back and opened the door.

Mr. White was waiting for me. He was still alone. "We understand this wasn't your choice. That's correct, isn't it?"

My flesh raised with a sudden chill. "That's right."

"Good," he said, lips drawn tight and thin with his smile.

"What's going to happen to Johnnie?"

Mr. White offered me his hand and helped me step down from the examination table. "He'll be reduced to a one or two, of course. Put to manual labor. If he keeps himself clean, he could even work back up to a four or five."

I knew Johnnie wouldn't want me to live that way.

"Of course your marriage is annulled. You're free to choose whomever you'd like to replace him from the other eights or nines."

"Replace him?"

Mr. White grimaced. "I'm sorry, I'm afraid I'm not terribly good with certain social graces. Please forgive me. Of course you'll want to take some time to yourself. But when you're ready, choose who you will."

By the time we walked outside, the Constables had Johnnie packed into a separate transport and were pulling out into traffic. I watched them drive away, wondering if I'd ever see him again. Either way, I knew he'd want me to take care of our baby. "Mr. White?" I asked, my senses beginning to return. "Can you tell me anything about the flag? It seems like I deserve to know something."

"What flag, dear?"

"The flag on my baby, of course."

"There is no flag on your baby. You made your sacrifice, just as Central predicted you would."

"You mean . . ."

Mr. White chuckled. "Of course we knew what your husband would do. Central is over ninety-nine percent accurate, remember. We don't question its results." My transport pulled up to the curb and Mr. White helped me inside. "Central," he said, "take the lady home. She's had a hard night."

"Mr. White?" I asked. "One last thing?"

He folded his hands in front of him. "Yes?"

"My baby? Can you give me any hint about what makes him so important?"

Mr. White glanced over his shoulder, and then leaned into the car. "I can't be specific, you know that, right?"

"Of course."

"Let's just say that I wouldn't be surprised to see him in Human Services."

That I *hadn't* expected. "Human Services?"

"Well, look at it this way, dear. He's already uncovered one traitor to the State, and he hasn't even been born yet." He then leaned back, with that tight, thin smile still stretched across his face, and slammed shut the door.

The transport sped away, whisking me home.

There was no driver.

Central was in control.

TRIAD IN THE KEY OF LIES

The first time she visited, the weather was nothing like the day we met. The late autumn winds hummed a dirge through the trees just outside my window, heralding the start of the rainy season. She looked at me, her clothes blood-stained, shredded and asked, "Did I do something wrong?"

"Don't worry about it," I said. I cinched down on the belt around her shoulder. Pebbles from the highway bit into my knees but I didn't feel them; I was too busy trying to keep her attention focused on me. Shattered glass and twisted metal surrounded the scorched blacktop; the smell of burnt rubber filled the air. Just minutes before I had been thinking how lovely the day was; the sky blue as innocence, the sun warm as forgiveness. The convertible ahead of me spoke of summer, the driver allowing her hand to twist and turn in the breeze outside the window while her hair blew back behind her like tails on a kite. She looked in the rear-view mirror and saw me behind her as the car drifted closer to the concrete barrier to her left. She corrected, looked back again; drifted. She focused on the light bar and the black-and-white of my patrol car. She had it: Blue light fever.

I reached for my mike and flipped on my p.a. even though I knew I wouldn't make it in time.

The barrier shredded most of it, but what remained of her arm slammed into my windshield like a rotted persimmon. She flew clear of the vehicle on the first roll, clouds of crimson mist spraying the air.

I ran to her, wanting instead to run away from the disfigurement before me, and saw God had decided to be particularly cruel that day.

She was still alive.

"Did I do something wrong?" she asked.

The second time she visited, I was still drunk. The room had just stopped spinning and I needed to sleep. Roll call was in five hours. My shorts smelled of piss. It was the tail end of my career, but I didn't know it. That's not true. Maybe I did know it. I just didn't care.

She stared at me and pointed toward her missing arm. "I think I broke my wrist," she said. "I think it might be bad."

"It's not as bad as all that," I said. The ambulance was on the way. Even though I knew it was pointless, I worked at keeping her eyes open and fixed on me. Shards of jagged bone peeked out from her shoulder joint, unnaturally white within the open wound like a wedding dress afloat on a sea of blood; a consummation of life and death.

Mere moments before she'd been the epitome of joy and beauty.

I'd followed her, powerless to stop myself. The wind rushed her beauty along the breeze behind her, filling my eyes with flowers freshly bloomed, my nose with roses of hope, my mind with thorns of desire. I pulled closer, to better see, anxious to take in as much of her as possible.

That was when she looked back, and her car began to drift.

The third time she visited me, her eyes blazed with rage. The steel tasted bitter in my mouth. "It's honeysuckle," she said. "Peaches and berries and white chocolate. You'll be okay. You're going to be fine."

We both knew she was lying.

We stared at each other. "I'm going to be okay?" she pleaded. "Tell me I'm going to be okay."

Death claimed her minutes before. Her body just didn't know it.

"Yes," I told her. "You're going to be fine."

The last thing she ever heard was a lie. She died in my arms, the falsehood still lingering in her ears.

"Did I do anything wrong?" she asked me.

"Don't worry about that now," I replied. "Will I be okay?" I asked, squeezing the trigger.

"You'll be fine," she lied.

I guess that's fair.

THE LAST VIEWING

Act I

It wasn't working. In spite of the pervasive sweet-cream scent of the popcorn, in spite of the twin two hundred pound waves of crushed rose velvet that eased back from the front of the silver screen; in spite of it all, nothing could fill the seat to Richard Dhoore's right. It was Catherine's seat, on the aisle, and it would remain as vacant and cool as the left side of his queen-sized bed.

Catherine had loved the Bijou. They spent many evenings here, catching a new action-adventure or squeezing in one of the Bijou's silent film nights when the Allen digital organ blossomed to full volume in concert with the action on the screen. It was their place.

Why he thought that a simple evening out would do any good Richard couldn't fathom. Friendly fire had created many holes in his life, and the empty seat next to him was just one more.

I'm a war widower.

For so many, the Bijou meant healing and community. The theatre opened back in 1937 and stayed in business for all but three of the intervening years. Three generations of young lovers had necked in the back row of this theatre, tasting the same juicy-fruit flavored kisses. Three generations of boys had excited at the caress of a girlfriend's head on their shoulder.

But Richard sat alone. He had a neatly folded American flag at home to comfort him, and a letter from George Bush, and nothing else. Even Sasia, his German shepherd, stood at the door after he returned at night, staring and waiting.

He slipped the cool paper of his Pepsi cup from the cup holder and took a sip to wash away the lump in his throat. Richard slid down in his seat, and prayed for the movie to make him forget.

The woman sat in Catherine's seat about one-third of the way through the movie. Her ankle-length wool skirt scratched against the cloth fabric of the chair as she sat down. The silk of her long-sleeved blouse caressed Richard's forearm as she brushed against him.

Lilacs danced from her pores.

Richard sat up straight, crossed his right leg over his left, and folded his hands in his lap. It was romance night at the Bijou, and on the screen Tom Hanks argued with his son about going to New York.

Breath warmed his ear. "I just love Jimmy Stewart, don't you?" she asked, her voice a melodic whisper.

Jimmy Stewart? Richard twisted his head and questioned her with his eyes. Now that he faced her, Richard realized that she was much younger than he thought. Her hair tried to stay in its bun, but here and there a tress of raven hair twisted free and lounged against the back of her neck. Her nose dipped upward at the tip, and her chin pointed a touch harder than it should, but that didn't hide her beauty. Like him, she wore a simple gold band on her left ring finger.

Richard turned back toward the screen. He hated it when people talked during the movie. And why did she have to sit next to him, anyway? There were plenty of open seats. He crossed his arms and pushed himself back into his chair, as if somehow doing so would make himself disappear entirely.

"Did I miss much?" she asked.

Richard shook his head. *If she opens her mouth again, I'm moving.* He moved his drink to the holder on his left.

She took the hint. She laced her fingers together and stared silently at the screen.

Soon, Richard again lost himself in the movie. This time, it was Meg Ryan's turn to complain. He always liked Meg Ryan, something he'd admitted to Catherine but to not many others. There was something believable; something that reminded you very much of a little sister. Something--

Richard's lost his attention as he felt fingers slip around his bicep. He looked over just in time to see the woman rest her blushing cheek against his shoulder.

Richard opened his mouth, then closed it again and grimaced. He wanted to tell her to let go and sit up. He wanted to tell her to leave him alone. He wanted to tell her to get the hell out of Catherine's seat.

He couldn't.

She looked so peaceful, resting there. The images on the screen flickered in her hazel eyes. *God, she looks a lot like Catherine.*

Guilt poisoned the moment. *She's dead, Richard. She's been dead a year now.* It didn't matter. Catherine was his wife. He still said his part of their goodnight, even to this day. He would lie there in the dark, waiting for Catherine's whisper, "Good night, my love," which never came. Richard heard it anyway. He'd answer, "Good night, my sweet," and until he said it, breaking the looming silence in the bedroom, Richard couldn't sleep. She still carried his love.

"Miss?" Richard said. He pulled her fingers from his arm and said it louder, "Miss?"

When she looked up, Richard watched as tears fled from her eyes. She stood and bolted up the aisle.

"Damn it," he said, and ran after her. He hit the lobby only a few seconds after her and the light hit his eyes like a flashbulb. Richard blinked twice, but when his eyes cleared, the woman was gone.

Devin--the half-owner of the theatre--stood behind the counter and stared at Richard. His forehead wrinkled with confusion. "You okay?" Devin asked.

Richard walked out the front door. Highway 101 ran directly in front of the Bijou, stretching from Anchorage on his right and Tijuana on his left. Summer still ruled supreme and the setting sun glared at him from above the westward buildings. That, and the combination of the salt-water breeze made Richard sneeze three times in rapid-fire succession. Tourists crowded the narrow sidewalks, some pointing into the windows of nearby shops, others just enjoying a late evening walk.

But she was gone.

Richard turned around and pulled his ticket-stub free from his pocket before he realized that the window was empty. Comedy and Tragedy mocked him from the ticket-booth wall. Richard pulled open the door and stepped back inside the Bijou.

The lobby was empty, except for Devin who looked up from behind the candy counter.

Richard eased up to the counter. "Sorry about that," he said.

Devin stared at him. "Sorry about what?"

Richard cheeks warmed. "I didn't mean to cause a scene. I just wanted to--" he didn't say the word apologize, "--to see if she was okay."

Devin grabbed a cup from the steel feeder. He filled it with ice and topped the glass with water. "Drink," he said.

Richard took a long sip. The ice hurt his teeth.

"Now who, pray tell, are you talking about?"

"That girl," Richard said. "The one that ran out of here."

Devin let out a short whistle. "I must have missed her, then."

Richard set the cup down. *He doesn't believe me.* "You didn't see a girl run out of here?" He asked. "Long skirt? Hair in a bun?"

Devin shook his head. "Nope," he said.

Richard blinked. His tongue found the roof of his mouth. He took a deep breath, tasting the alcohol of Devin's cologne, then said, "No matter." He fished in his pants pocket, pulled out his keys and turned toward the front door.

"Aren't you going to stay for the rest of the movie?" Devin called after him.

Richard turned and faced him. "I'm tired. I think I'll just go home and sleep," he said.

"Too much movie magic for one night?"

"No," said Richard. "I know how it ends."

Act II

He didn't go out again until the next Wednesday. It wasn't that he wanted to see her again, he really didn't, but well, he did still owe her an apology. If she happened to be there, then so be it. If not . . .

He got there early. The torchlights on the sides of the theater cast half circle shadows on the ceiling and a hundred shades of red closed in on him from all sides. Music played softly over the speaker system: Rachmaninov's "Variations on a Theme," by Paganini. Richard craned his neck around toward the entrances. A handful of patrons peppered the theater, none closer than necessary to the next. The theater manager announced the movie--the Bijou was once place the tradition had never left--and the house lights went down. *Fade to black.*

Richard moved his drink to the left side cup holder and settled in to his seat.

She sat down next to him. She wore the same clothes, but Richard thought she might be wearing just a touch more perfume. She held a large brown paper sack full of popcorn. Richard smiled in spite of himself.

He leaned over and said, "I'm sorry about the other night."

She turned her head and their eyes met. She didn't say a word, smiled, and leaned against his shoulder.

They watched the movie. On the screen, Christopher Reeves and Jane Seymour glided along a lake in a rowboat. Christopher Reeves whistled.

"Thank you," she said.

Richard stole two kernels of her popcorn. "I don't even know your name," he said.

She tilted her head so that he could see her face. "I'm Elyse," she said, her smile soft. "Don't you just love Robert Mitchum?"

"Elyse." Richard closed his eyes and thought of Catherine.

The movie ended, and the few patrons around them left at the first sign of the credits. The house lights eased up to a fraction of their full potential.

It seemed to Richard as if everyone who walked up the aisle stared directly at the two of them and Richard felt an unfamiliar warmth in his cheeks. He pulled his hand free from Elise's grip and started to stand.

"Not yet," Elyse said. "Just till the end of the credits. Please?"

Richard eased back into his chair.

What was he doing here, anyway? If one of Catherine's friends happened to walk in, he'd never be able to show his face around town again. *It's been a year, though! Am I supposed to just curl up and die?*

Elyse squeezed his arm. "I just wanted to say thank you again," she said. "Since my husband died, I haven't had anyone around. I know it's a bit peculiar."

Her voice, now that she didn't have to whisper, contained a musical quality. It reminded Richard of wind chimes. "I'm sorry," he said. "How long has it been?"

"Just over a year now. He was killed in the war."

Richard held her hand. She relaxed a bit, he saw, but her posture never changed. She sat straight. Richard found it very feminine; elegant even. "That's hard," he said. "I know."

The credits ended and the house lights came up full.

From the back of the theater, Devin's voice called, "You about done in there?"

Elyse looked at Richard and said, "I have to go anyway. I have an early morning."

"Yeah," he said. "Me too."

Elyse grimaced. "There's a war on, you know."

That was odd, Richard thought, but before he could say anything, she stood and slung her handbag over her shoulder. "Next Wednesday?" She asked.

"Sure thing."

"I think they're showing a Betty Gable film," she said, then turned and hurried up the aisle.

Richard followed behind her, but she was gone before he reached the lobby.

"Did you enjoy the movie?" Devin asked, pausing his sweeping when he saw .

"Yeah."

Devin looked over both shoulders before he said, "I can't stand the tear-jerkers. But they sell the tickets, you know?"

If the ten people in the audience were an indication of "selling tickets," Richard didn't want to think about what sales were like for an unpopular film.

"See you next week?" Devin asked.

"Wouldn't miss it for the world."

"Gotta love that movie magic."

Richard smiled.

Indeed.

ACT III

To Richard the next week crept by as if he were waiting for a cast to be removed so he could scratch the tender skin underneath. When Wednesday finally rolled back around, Richard stood at the ticket window fifteen minutes before the theater opened. He bought a super-sized drink and an assortment of candies and made his way to his seat.

He looked around the theatre. The handful of patrons all seemed to have come from the same dinner party. An usher stood in the aisle, a pillbox hat crooked slightly on his head. They cleaned the place up, Richard thought. Funny he hadn't noticed before. Even the organ looked polished.

A man in a tuxedo walked to the front of the audience and announced the movie. *Hmm. I wonder where Devin is tonight?*

The house lights faded, and Richard settled in for the show. By the time Elyse arrived, he had finished a third of his drink. The scent of sour apples drifted past his nose from the open box of candy in his lap.

She changed her makeup, Richard thought. Her cheeks look like they've just been pinched. On her head rested a small, black hat with a white lace veil that hung almost to her eyebrows.

In the front row, someone lit a cigarette.

Elyse's hand slid around his arm and she rested against his shoulder. "Don't you just love Humphrey Bogart?" she asked.

Richard waved his hand in front of his face. "God I wish someone would throw that jerk out."

Elyse giggled. "Oh, Richard. You're such a prude," she said.

On the screen, Harrison Ford and Anne Heche were sitting in a smoky bar while a black man played the piano. Richard squeezed his eyes shut and shook his head.

"So," Elyse asked, "what's your deal, anyway?"

Richard looked her in the eye. She looked positively ravishing. Richard hadn't felt this good in a long time. He hadn't known it was possible. Still, there was something odd about Elyse, beyond the obvious fact that she was terrible with the names of actors, that is. "What do you mean?" Richard said.

"I mean," she said, "how is it that you can be here?" Elyse tilted her head in astonishment. "You know."

Richard didn't know, but they could figure it out later, after the movie. He thought that tonight, they might go for dinner after. "Shh," Richard said. "I want to watch the movie."

Elyse sighed and rested her head on his shoulder. Tonight the scent was patchouli. The stiff white lace on her hat poked his shoulder.

On the screen, Humphrey Bogart and Anne Heche smoldered with chemistry.

What the . . .

The usher lit a match for a man in the third row.

Richard closed his eyes. He didn't want to believe what was becoming clear. The past was catching up with him.

Catherine. Richard let his mind slip into places he'd avoided for over a year.

Her hair smelled like guava, always. She stuttered as a child, and every once in a while, she would slip back into it and would tease her for days. She used to laugh right along with him. He used to rest his head in the crook of her shoulder when they lied down for the night, and she would rock gently. Most nights, he'd fall asleep there and she would have to wake him and make him roll over. And she'd sing. Oh, how she would sing. He'd be working in the living room and she'd shut herself away in the back room so as not to disturb him, and she would sing for hours. It wasn't in the least disturbing. On the other hand, he never did get much work done during those times. He couldn't help but listen. Then she left for Iraq when her Guard unit got called up for active duty. She was a nurse, and she loved it. She didn't need to work, but she wanted to help, anyway. Then the day her medical supply truck found its way in front of a rocket propelled grenade and the firefight erupted and then the bullet, and the phone call.

The phone call.

It was his own favorite movie, and in spite of how many times he watched it, the ending didn't change.

"Elyse," Richard said, his eyes still tightly closed. "Where did your husband die?"

Silence.

"Elyse?"

"Normandy," she said.   Her grip tightened on his arm. "Richard, I'm so glad you have flat feet."

 Richard opened his eyes.

On the screen, Lauren Bacall boarded an airplane while Humphrey Bogart watched.

On the screen, Anne Heche boarded an airplane while Harrison Ford watched.

"This isn't going to work, Elyse." Richard said.

Richard felt her fingernails biting into his flesh. "Of course it will," Elyse said. "Just let it happen."

Oh God, Catherine. I miss you so much.   Richard peeled her hands from his arm. He looked into her eyes. "We can't see each other any more," he said.

"Why?" She asked. Her cheeks were ashen. The patchouli had faded and lilacs bloomed anew.

"You know why.   Time only goes one way, Elyse."   The blue entrails of smoke from the front row faded, the stale odor vanishing. "I'm through trying to live backwards," Richard said. "Movies end and new ones begin, like memories. You can't just replace the actors."

She stood.

Off the screen, Elyse was crying.

She walked three rows up the aisle, turned, and said, "Goodbye, my love."

Richard turned away and didn't look back.

Through the blur, Richard watched as Anne Heche ran across the tarmac and into Harrison Ford's arms. The sunset behind them, they kissed.

The end credits rolled, and Richard watched the audience file out one by one. He breathed a sigh of relief as a teenage boy wearing an Old Navy fleece pullover walked past him.

"Richard," Richard said, "this could be the start of a beautiful friendship."

Swell music.

Fade to black.

The Bijou looked the same as Richard remembered. Faded? Maybe. Well loved? Absolutely. He stepped into the lobby and saw Devin standing behind the counter.

"Like the movie?" Devin asked.

"It wasn't bad," Richard said.

Devin grabbed a popcorn bag and filled it with a scoop from the well. He set it on the counter between them and popped a few kernels into his mouth. "Next Wednesday, then?" He asked.

"We'll see." Richard said. "I may have had my fill for a while."

Devin frowned. "You can never watch too many movies."

"Maybe you're right. But next week," Richard said, "I think I'll take the aisle seat."

Devin smiled. "You know," he said, "That might not be a bad idea."

Richard nodded, then grabbed a handful of popcorn for himself. He tossed a kernel into the air and caught it in his mouth. "Goodnight, Devin."

"Did you get your movie magic?" Devin asked.

Richard turned and left without saying a word.

COPPER ANGELS

1.

The lady Deke was nice. She had pretty hair like mommy's, only not as bright. Mommy's hair shined like it had a little bit of the sun in it. Well, it used to. Mommy didn't wash her hair as much anymore. Not after that time she fell down.

I didn't know what to do, and I was sad that Mommy got scared by the Dekes, but they tell us at school that if something isn't right you have to tell a Deke about it. Sometimes they were scary; all dressed up in all that plasticy stuff they wear and a big black sunglass that comes down from their helmets so you can't see their eyes. But this lady wasn't like that. She wore a long black dress and I could see my reflection in her shoes. She smelled like nice soap.

"Is Mommy going to be okay?" I asked her.

She smiled at me and put her fingers together, like a church steeple. There was a desk in her office, but she didn't sit behind it to talk to me. She sat in a chair right next to me and stroked my hair. It felt nice. "Your Mommy is going to be fine, Mary. They're both going to be fine."

"Where's Daddy?" I asked. He wasn't home when the Dekes came.

"Your Daddy is in the next room. We're talking to him about your Mommy now." She picked up a tape player from her desk and pushed a button. "Do you mind if I ask you some questions?" she asked.

I shook my head. I had to explain, after all.

"You're a good girl, Mary," she said. I wasn't afraid at all. She had a picture of Jesus on her wall and other than the desk the office reminded me of Daddy's office at home. "How old are you, Mary?"

"I'm almost seven. But I'm in the third grade already." I knew I shouldn't brag, but I had to tell the whole truth to a Deke. "Mommy says sometimes being too smart isn't the best thing, but God made me smart so that I could learn to be a better person."

"I'm sure that's just what He did, honey. And you know what?" she asked.

I shook my head no.

"It worked," she said.

I smiled at her. She was really nice.

"So why did you call us?" she asked.

It got real quiet all of a sudden. I could hear the hum of the tape recorder. "I was afraid the man from under the ground was going to stop the Angel from coming," I told her. "Daddy wasn't home, so I called the Dekes--" I covered my mouth when I realized what I said, but the words were already out. "I'm sorry," I said. "I didn't mean to . . ."

The Deke lady just smiled at me. "It's okay honey," she said, and she rubbed my arm. Her hands were so soft. "I've heard it before. Don't worry about that now. Why don't you start from the beginning, okay?"

"Okay," I said.

So I told her about the time Mommy fell down.

2.

" . . .Barthomew, Thomas, Matthew, James, Simon, Labbaeus and . . .um . . ."

"Judas," Mommy said.

I never had been good at history, but Mommy always helped me whenever we had the chance. On the day she fell down, we were going over schoolwork while we rode into town for Mommy's meeting with Daddy's boss. She looked real pretty that day. She had on a new skirt that Daddy said was too short for her, but I thought it looked good. Her hair was bright and shiny blonde in the warm sunshine, like Jesus' hair, and she had it braided around her head like a queen's crown.

We were in the new electric car, so we didn't have to shout or anything to hear each other.

"I always forget Judas!" I said.

Mommy smiled at me and her eyes were blue, so I knew she was happy. Whenever Mommy gets mad, her eyes turn bright green. "Most people wish they could," she said. It was a grown-up joke, so I didn't get it, but I laughed anyway. Since daddy got his promotion, we could afford a tutor, but Mommy said she liked helping me herself. Daddy kept trying to get her to hire a saved-maid, too, but Mommy said she didn't want some harlot running around her house.

We pulled up next to a restaurant just before you cross the bridge into town, where they make the cheesy-bread. Anyway, Mommy told me to wait in the car 'cause she was only going to be a minute or two. Mr. Alpheus had left his ring at our house the last time he was over for dinner 'cause he took it off when he washed his hands and forgot to put it back on. He called Mommy that morning and asked if she could bring it over to him where he was having lunch.

Mommy leaned over and gave me a kiss on the cheek, then went inside.

She was in there for a long time, but I stayed put, like I was supposed to. Mommy left the keys in the car so I could listen to the radio if I wanted, but I just watched all the people driving by instead. I started to get dizzy from moving my head back and forth and trying to see people's faces as they sped by, so I stared at the angels on the bridge for a while. I always liked those angels. They're so shiny, like an old republic penny when it's brand new. I figured that's what they made them out of anyway. Bunches of old republic pennies. They weren't much good for anything else, anymore. Why not make angels out of them?

I was trying to figure out how many pennies it took to make each one when I heard the car door open. Mommy climbed into her seat.

Her hair hung down onto her shoulders, but bunches of it were still tangled from where she had her braids in. Her knees were all scraped up and bright red, like when you skin yourself but not enough to bleed? And her shirt was torn.

I got real scared. Mommy's eyes were bright green and she had tears in them.

"What happened, Mommy?" I asked.

Mommy looked at me like she hadn't known I was there. She tried to smile, but it didn't stay on her face very long. "I just fell down," she said. But her voice was funny, like she had a cold or something. "Fell down real hard."

I went to hug her, 'cause I know when I fall down the best thing in the world is a hug, but Mommy jerked away from me. Her lips opened a little bit, like she was surprised, but then she started crying harder and hugged me for a long time.

"It's okay," I said. "We'll go home and put band-aids on it and you'll be all better, okay?"

She just kept hugging me. After a long time, I started wondering if the people passing by could see us and what they thought. Mommy was a much bigger crybaby about falling down than I was, that's for sure.

A long time later, Mommy let go and started the car. We drove straight home. She didn't talk to me any more that day.

3.

The lady Deke crossed her arms. "What happened when you got home?" she asked. Her lips got real small while she waited for me to answer.

"Nothing, really," I said. It's wasn't exactly the whole truth but I couldn't figure out how to explain it very well. Mommy just started acting strange, is all.

"Well . . .did she help you with any more of your homework that day?"

I shook my head. The lady Deke smiled at me and pointed to the tape recorder. "No," I said, pointing my mouth toward the microphone. "She just went home and then took a bath."

The lady Deke tilted her head and squinted her eyes together. "Really? She didn't do anything else?"

I didn't understand why Mommy did what she did that day, but I got the idea that I'd better tell the Deke anyway.

4.

Well Mommy came right home and took a bath. She told me to go play upstairs for a little while and her voice sounded like it probably wasn't a good idea to tell her that I really didn't want to. I didn't have anything I really wanted to play with, but I went upstairs anyway and drew in my notebook for a while.

I couldn't stop thinking about the shiny angels on the bridge, so I started drawing angels. I must have drawn eight or nine angels with swords in their hands like you always see, but after a while that got old so I started drawing them bringing new babies down from heaven.

Each one I drew kept getting better and better, but I knew I had to use the colored pencils if I was going to get it right. Mommy always talked about how maybe one day I'd get a baby brother, so I started drawing them real carefully. I thought if I drew the angel perfect with a little blue bundle in his arms, and the drew Mommy and Daddy and me down on earth waiting for him . . . It's silly, I know. But I drew it perfect anyway. Daddy always told me how happy Mommy was all the time when I was a baby. If God sent Mommy another baby, she could be twice as happy. To tell the truth though, I really wanted a little brother. I love playing with Mommy, but sometimes I wish I had a brother to play with when Mommy had to do grown-up things. I held the picture in my hands and prayed. Not for me, but for Mommy and then, at just that moment, the sun came out from behind the clouds and shined in through my bedroom window.

I carefully tore the page from my notebook and took it downstairs to show Mommy. I got down the first three stairs and was just about to call for Mommy when I saw her crouched down beside the fireplace.

It was the middle of the day, and it was hot out too, but Mommy was building a fire. I couldn't figure out why she would want to do that, but I didn't want to upset her, so I just watched.

She just got the fire going good and that's when she started acting really strange. She pulled a bundle of clothes out from under her bathrobe and threw them on top of the fire. I tiptoed down the steps until I could see past her shoulder.

It was her new dress and blouse she'd just bought. The one Daddy didn't like.

I wanted to ask her like a hundred questions, but I couldn't figure out which one to ask first, so I just went back upstairs.

I hung my picture above the pillows on my bed.

Mommy could see it later. When she felt better.

5.

"How long did she continue to act like that?" the Deke lady asked me. She was leaning in close again. She smiled as she talked, but it looked like she didn't really want to be smiling.

"Well, she got mad at me later but she was better after Daddy came home."

The Deke lady tilted her head. "She got mad at you?" she asked. "Why?"

I didn't want to talk about it, but I didn't have much choice.

6.

Mommy put on one of her nice Sunday dresses after she finished making the fire. She called me down from upstairs when lunch was ready. Usually she makes me a hot lunch on the days that Daddy's at work and I don't have school--I'm in a special class and only go to school three days a week--but that day I remember she just made me two pieces of toast and poured me a glass of orange juice. I kept waiting for her to pull macaroni and cheese out of the oven or to open a can of ravioli or something, but she just stood over me and said, "Eat."

She looked really mad so I didn't question her. I'm not supposed to question her anyway. That's what improper little boys and girls do, so I try not to do that. Mommy crossed her arms and it looked for a minute like she was going to start crying, but she just turned around and left me alone in the kitchen. She *never* does that. Even if she doesn't eat with me she always sits down at the table and talks to me while I have lunch.

I figured she was just mad because she ruined her new clothes when she fell down and had to burn them. It sure would have made me mad. I figured I'd just better leave her alone for a little bit.

I said grace and then finished both pieces of toast pretty quick but I was still hungry so I got up and opened the 'fridge to see if there was something in there that I knew how to make for myself. I had just decided to have one of Mommy's yummy yogurts and was reaching for it when I heard Mommy yell something bad. I'd tell you what she said, but I'm not allowed to say words like that.

I ran back over to the table without the yogurt and sat down with my back straight like I'm supposed to. I heard her run down the stairs and before I knew it she came into the kitchen. She was crying, but it was angry crying. Her face was really red and she kept taking short breaths through her nose. She slammed down my picture of the angel on the table. She yelled, "What's this?"

I didn't know what I'd done wrong, so I just shrugged my shoulders.

"You want a baby brother?" She asked. "Is that it?"

I shrugged my shoulders again. Mommy stared at me for a long time. I just kept my eyes on the plate full of breadcrumbs. I didn't want to make her any more mad on accident. Finally, she picked up the picture and started tearing it into little pieces.

I couldn't believe she was doing that. It was so mean and Mommy was never mean, except when I did something really bad, but this wasn't bad so I didn't understand why she was so upset. It felt like someone had just hit me in the tummy. I thought for sure that Mommy didn't really love me any more.

When she finished tearing up my picture she stared right into my eyes and said, "Don't make wishes for things you don't understand."

Then she threw the pieces of paper into the garbage under the sink. "You just sit here at the table until I tell you to get up again."

I sat there for at least an hour until I finally had to pee so bad that I couldn't wait any longer. I was scared to ask her if I could get up, but I knew she'd be even madder if I peed my pants at the table.

"When you're done," Mommy called to me from the other room, "go upstairs and play. I'm still upset with you."

So I did. I grabbed the pieces of my picture from the trashcan and stuffed them in my pockets.

7.

"Why did you do that?" the lady Deke asked me. "Your mother just tore up your picture. She obviously didn't want it around. Weren't you afraid you'd get into trouble?"

"Yeah, kind of." I said. "But I thought that maybe this was one of those times that Mommy was just in a bad mood and would say she was sorry after she got over being mad." That didn't happen too often, but sometimes it did. It was the only thing I could think of that made sense. I really didn't do anything wrong.

"Sometimes parents do that, honey," the lady Deke said. "It's not easy to be a Mommy sometimes."

"Yeah."

"But you say she got better when your father came home?"

"Uh-huh."

"What happened?"

"Well," I said. "She was just, you know, happy. But it was weird, too."

"How so?"

I tried to figure out the best way to explain it. "Well, it was like she was *really* happy, you know? Like it was Christmas or Easter or something."

The lady Deke crossed her arms and tilted her head to the side. "She burned her new clothes, yelled at you for drawing an angel, and then she was happy again when your father came home?"

"Uh-huh," I said. "She really loves Daddy. Daddy's a very important person, did you know that? He works for the Ministry of Prevention and he--"

"I know who your father is, sweetie. Let's get back to your mother."

"Okay."

"Did she stay happy?"

I shook my head, and then remembered the tape recorder. "No, she didn't."

8.

She was fine until Malachai, Daddy's driver, showed up to take him to work. As soon as he left, Mommy went into the living room and called Elizabeth, her friend from next door. "Come over," Mommy said. "It's important." And then she started crying again. She hung up the phone and saw me standing there.

She didn't smile at all. "Upstairs until I tell you to come down," she said. I must have sulked because Mommy yelled, "Now!"

I ran up the stairs as fast as I could and slammed my bedroom door behind me. I waited for Mommy to come up and scold me for that, but after five minutes or so hiding under my covers I figured that she wasn't coming.

I reached under my mattress and pulled out the pieces of my drawing. I had some scotch tape with my school stuff, so I got that out and started to tape my picture back together.

I did a good job, too. It was almost perfect. In one or two spots you could see the rough part of the paper, where it had been torn, but it wasn't too bad at all. I slid the picture back under my mattress and I was trying to figure out what to do next when I heard the doorbell ring.

I tiptoed over to my door and opened it a crack.
Mommy was at the front door and I heard her talking to someone. It was Elizabeth. "Hi Honey, you sounded like . . .oh God, what happened?"

Mommy was crying again. In between sobs she said, "In the den."

I waited a couple of minutes before I went downstairs.

9.

"You weren't afraid that you'd get in trouble?" the lady Deke asked.

I shook my head. "It didn't matter if I did," I said. "Mommy was sad and I didn't know why. I thought that if I could figure out even a little bit, then maybe I could help. I always made Mommy happy before, so I figured that I just didn't know what was wrong but if I did, I could help."

The lady Deke nodded and folded her hands in her lap. "I'm sorry, go on," she said.

10.

When I got down outside the door to the den, I heard Mommy crying some more. The door was open a bit, so I made sure that I stayed to the left side, so I wouldn't be seen. I peeked into the den and saw Elizabeth hugging Mommy.

She was stroking Mommy's hair and going, "Shh. Shh. It'll be okay, honey. It'll be okay."

Mommy was shaking her head. "And how is that?" she asked. "Tell me, how is it ever going to be okay again?"

They were quiet for a long time after that. Finally, Elizabeth said, "Alpheus, huh?" And then she called him some names I'm not allowed to say.

Mommy nodded.

"Now I understand why you did what you did. He's untouchable."

Mr. Alpheus always shook Daddy's hand and mussed my hair when he came over, so it didn't really make sense, but adults are strange sometimes.

"I may need you to do something for me," Mommy said.

Elizabeth pulled away from her then. She looked a little scared, actually. She mumbled for a minute and I couldn't understand what she said, but then I heard her say, "I don't really know what I could--"

Mommy interrupted her. She looked really mad again. "Don't play games with me, Elizabeth," she said. "Just understand that I may need you."

Elizabeth was chewing on her lower lip, but she didn't say anything back. She just nodded and squeezed her eyes shut real tight, then hugged Mommy again. After a while she said, "Let's cross that bridge when we come to it."

They talked a little bit more, but most of it I didn't understand. I think Mommy really hurt herself when she fell down, though.

She said something about being ripped.

11.

The lady Deke leaned forward in her chair. "Honey, this is very important," she said. "Okay?"

I nodded my head. I was a little afraid at how serious she looked.

"Do you know Elizabeth's last name? Where she lives?"

I told her. "But sometimes I think she lives someplace under the ground," I said.

The lady Deke tilted her head to the side. "You said that before, about the man you were afraid of. What do you mean she lives under the ground?"

"I heard Mommy and her talk about it the next time she came over."

"Okay," she said. "Take your time and tell me the rest."

12.

I still didn't understand what was wrong with Mommy. She acted happy whenever Daddy was around, but as soon as he'd leave she'd start getting strange again. Like once, when we were sitting in church, the preacher started telling the story about Jesus on the cross, when he doubted God, and I looked over at Mommy and there were tears in her eyes.

It's a sad story, but Mommy's heard it lots before so I couldn't figure out why she was crying over it now. When service was over, Mommy made Daddy hurry up and take us home.

It made Daddy a little mad 'cause he and Mommy normally stay around and shake hands with lots of people there afterwards, but Mommy didn't talk to anyone and she actually pulled away from one lady when she went to shake Mommy's hand.

When Mommy got home she threw up. Daddy stopped being mad when he realized she was sick, so everything was okay again. She got sick a lot, but most of the time it was when Daddy wasn't home.

She'd be really white in the morning, like when your stomach feels like it's full of butterflies or something?

But Daddy didn't seem to notice too much, or if he did, he didn't say anything. Besides, Mommy was happy whenever Daddy was around so I didn't want to say anything that might change that.

About a month after the last time Elizabeth came over, Mommy called her again. I heard Mommy yell at her on the phone, but I couldn't make out what she was saying.

I got sent to my room again, but I snuck down after Elizabeth got there. They didn't say anything to each other when Mommy opened the door. Elizabeth just came inside and the two of them went right to the den.

When I got close enough to hear them, Elizabeth was talking. "No, I can't."

Then, Mommy got real close to Elizabeth and whispered, but it wasn't like she was trying to tell her a secret or anything. It was scary. "Elizabeth," she said. "I know you can do this. I know that you know people. You're my friend and you're mostly harmless so I've ignored it. But if you don't do this for me, there'll be Dekes coming through your door before you get home."

Elizabeth stepped away from Mommy and crossed her arms. After a second, her head dipped and she started to shake a bit. "No one from the underground is going to touch this," she said. "Your husband is too powerful. It'll smell like a trap."

"Convince them," Mommy said. "And get me and Mary new traveling papers, just in case. You know I've got the money. I've loaned you enough in the past."

Elizabeth nodded. "Someone will be here tomorrow morning," she said. "Have the money ready. They'll bring your papers. You have pictures?"

Mommy nodded and handed Elizabeth an envelope. "There's twenty grand in there. There'll be twenty more tomorrow. It's more than the going rate. And Elizabeth?" Mommy said. "Don't even think about running. If someone isn't here tomorrow morning, my husband finds out about you. You can't get far enough away by then."

Elizabeth just stared at Mommy, then said, "When did you get so cold, anyway?"

Mommy didn't even move. "The minute that man put this thing in me," she said. "I want it out, understand?"

Elizabeth nodded, then turned to leave. I ran back to the stairs and up into my room.

13.

The lady Deke looked up as a young man opened the door to the office. He had on a very nice suit, but not near as nice as the ones Daddy has. "Yes Crawford?" she said.

The man glanced down at the floor for a minute, and then said, "I'm sorry to interrupt Deacon, but I thought you'd like to know that we picked up Ms. Bartlow at the Alabama border crossing . . .Elizabeth Bartlow? She was traveling under a false identity."

The Deke lady smiled, but her lips were real tight, you know? She said, "Thank you Crawford. Anything else?"

He shook his head and then left. He closed the door real soft.

"I'm sorry, honey," the Deke lady said. "Now tell me what happened this morning, and it's real important that you try hard to remember exactly what was said."

14.

Mommy got real upset this morning when I reminded her that school was cancelled today due to a teacher's conference. She knew about it for weeks, but sometimes she forgot to check the schedule. She was acting really weird, though. She tried to get Daddy to take me to work with him. She said she needed a day by herself.

But Daddy told Mommy that she knew he couldn't take me to work with him and Mommy giggled a bit and said, "Of course. I was just being silly. I thought I might do some shopping or something this morning."

And that really confused me, you know? 'cause I knew Mommy had someone coming over this morning to take the bad thing out of her. I felt a whole lot better, that's for sure. At least now I knew why Mommy had been so upset lately.

That happened all the time in the bible. Like when Jesus cast the evil spirits out of that man? Mommy just had something bad inside her and a good man was going to come over and take it out and Mommy would be okay again.

But then Mommy got really weird after Daddy left for work. She made me a huge breakfast. Eggs and bacon and pancakes and potatoes and milk. I ate as much as I could. I even made myself a little sick trying to clean my plate, but I couldn't finish everything. But instead of Mommy getting mad at me like she would sometimes when I didn't finish my meal, she just took the plate away and then walked me up to my room.

"Now listen and listen good," she said. "Do not come downstairs until I tell you to. Even if you get hungry or thirsty or anything, do you understand?"

I nodded. "Did I do something wrong?" I asked.

She shook her head, and it looked like she was going to start crying again. "Just don't come downstairs."

I nodded my head and Mommy closed my bedroom door as she left.

And I meant to keep my promise, too. I don't know why I didn't. I really don't. Mommy was going to be okay again and everything was going to be like it was but for some reason I just couldn't stop worrying about Mommy. What if the man hurt her when he was trying to take the bad thing out of her? What if he hurt her and then left and I couldn't come downstairs to help her because I'd promised not to?

So when I heard the doorbell ring, I made up my mind. I'd stand at the top of the stairs and listen. That way, I could hear if Mommy needed my help and called for me but I wouldn't be breaking my promise not to go downstairs? I knew that it was fibbing a little bit, but I just hoped that God would understand that it was because I loved my Mommy so much.

I didn't see the man come in the front door, but I heard his voice easy. He had a very deep voice, and it was scratchy, you know? After the front door closed I heard the man say, "Do you have the envelope?"

It was quiet for a minute, and then the man said, "I just want you to know that I'm only doing this because you were . . .well, you know. If this were under any other circumstances, I'd leave you to your fate. Your husband has hurt enough of my friends in the past that I still had to think twice about coming over here."

Mommy said, "I understand, and I'm sorry about your friends."

"Ma'am," the man said. "You'll forgive me if I don't believe that. We're standing here in this grand house and you've got two expensive cars and your husband travels to work every day in a chauffeur-driven limo and I really think that the only reason you'd even talk to someone like me is because of what's in it for you."

Mommy cleared her throat. "I see," she said. "Well then, you've made yourself perfectly clear. Is there anything else?"

It was quiet for what seemed like a long time, but it was probably only ten seconds or so. Then, the man said, really mean like, "I want to hear you say it."

Then Mommy said, "I don't want to have this baby."

15.

The lady Deke took my hands. "Now you're absolutely certain that's what she said?

I nodded my head up and down real hard. "Yeah, 'cause I got real scared then. I knew that the under ground man was going to try and stop the angel from bringing my baby brother down. I just couldn't figure out why Mommy was going to let him do it!"

"So you went into your Mommy and Daddy's room and called us?"

"Uh-huh. I was going to call Daddy but I couldn't remember his phone number at work. I just wanted to make sure that someone came and stopped the under ground man before he stopped the angel. Mommy was sick. She didn't know what she was doing. She wouldn't have let him into the house if she were well, I know that."

The lady Deke looked at me for a moment and then smiled. "You did the right thing, Mary. We got there in time. Your little brother is going to be just fine." She reached over and switched off the tape recorder.

"Is Mommy going to be okay? She's not in trouble, is she?"

The lady Deke stared at me for a while. "That's between her and God, sweetheart."

I was so glad to hear her say that. I knew that God would understand.

A few minutes later, another lady came into the office. She had on a long black dress, too, but she was older and her hair was tied back in a bun.

"This is Mrs. Overton, Mary. She's with child support services. You're going to stay at her home for a little bit while your Mommy gets better, okay?"

I nodded my head. Mrs. Overton took my hand and helped me out of my seat.

"Hold on a second," the lady Deke said. She stepped behind her desk, opened a drawer and pulled out a shiny Deke badge. "Here you go, Mary. You did a wonderful thing today. I hereby proclaim you an honorary Deacon."

I took the badge from her. She was such a nice lady. I know I shouldn't have, but I dropped Mrs. Overton's hand and then gave the lady Deke a hug.

She hugged me back.

16.

Mrs. Overton had a car waiting outside the Deke station. I looked back over my shoulder at the sign on the building.

Ministry of Prevention
Evangelical Fellowship of Atlanta
Child Protection Division

There was also a statue of the holy mother holding the baby Jesus in her arms. And angel sat in the air above them, protecting them with his sword. It made me smile.

At the bottom of the statue were the words:

For those we couldn't save.
May God grant mercy upon their souls.

I climbed into the back of the car with Mrs. Overton. I looked at the badge the lady Deke gave me and pinned it to the front of my shirt.

Everything was going to be okay now. Soon, my brother and Daddy and Mommy and me would all be together again, and Mommy would be well. I knew that because the lady Deke told me so, and because I knew that Jesus would make sure of it.

God would understand.

He always understood.

MALINGERING

I didn't notice Billy standing there until I had the front side of the Mustang jacked up and the driver's side tire removed. He was outgrowing his clothes again. I'd have to do something about that soon. Since the oil peak and subsequent crash in the early nineties, I'd become quite the tailor. Who could afford to buy clothes anymore? One day, demand simply outran supply and there was only so much oil to begin with. The collapse of society started soon after.

Some said we had twenty years. Some said fifty.

"Stand back, son," I told Billy, scanning the edge of the tree-line for any movement. It wasn't always safe outside. You never knew when or where scavengers would show up anymore.

"Uh-huh," Billy said. He retreated a couple of inches, almost knocking over the portable scanner in the process. It'd been blessedly silent so far today.

"Watch your step," I said, glancing at him. "What are you doing out here?" Billy rarely left the confines of the basement and the puzzles of his chemistry set, particularly when I was working. You'd think that he could discover an alternate energy source and save the planet all by himself from watching him work. Part of me wanted to be angry with him for leaving his mother alone in the house, but that wasn't really fair so I let it go.

"I don't know," he said. It's always been tough for my boy to talk to me. I don't know why. It's not like I treat him badly or beat him, God forbid. Sometimes he'd walk around the house for days looking like he had a piece of paper on the tip of his tongue that he was afraid to spit out.

"Well then, give me a hand," I said. "Hand me those pliers." Billy spun around a couple of times, his chin to his chest, and finally bent over and picked up the pliers. I held out my hand and he set the cool steel in my palm.

"Dad?"

"Yes?" The once silver discus of the rotor had rusted to a burnt orange circle. I removed the retaining pins from the sideways stretched horseshoe of metal that held the brake pads in place.

"Why was Mom yelling last night?"

I knew this was coming, I just didn't know when. "Hand me those pads, will you?"

Billy's chin went back into his chest.

How am I supposed to tell my son that his mother is . . .well, no longer herself? How do you tell your son that his mother's brain is slowly eating itself away with cancer? He had enough to worry about as it was. With the food shortage, Billy didn't even have a one-in-fifteen chance of making it to adulthood and he knew it. When oil prices went sky high, food prices went with them. A six-year old shouldn't have to worry about starving to death or planet-wide oil wars or being shot for a bag of potatoes. He shouldn't have to watch his mother slowly die in front of his eyes.

"The white box. With the blue stripes," I said.

He found it.

I slipped the first pad from the caliper, easing the kidney shaped piece of metal from its resting-place next to the rotor.

Billy handed me the box. "Dad?"

"Your mother is sick," I said. I opened the box and pulled out a new pad. It seemed such a waste to put new anything on this car, but I had saved up enough gas to get us out east, away from the coast. I heard that farming communities were forming all over the middle states and if the Chinese hit the coast and went after the pipeline, I wanted to be long gone. I just prayed that a man with a sick wife and a little boy would be accepted there. In this new world, everyone had to pull their own weight. I had to hope that there was compassion left out there somewhere. That is, if the car even made it that far.

"There's something wrong with her brain." I pushed back on the piston that shoved the pads together, creating space for the new pad.

"Oh," he said. Billy squatted down next to my open toolbox and started pushing the tools around.

I slipped the new pad into place and wiped the grease on the leg of my jeans. Normally Cheryl would kill me for that, but under the circumstances . . .

"Dad?"

"Damn." The second pad was stuck. I wiggled it back and forth. "What, Billy?"

"Do you think that doctors could fix her?"

The pad popped loose. It was warm to the touch. "I don't know, son. Even if we found a doctor that would barter, I don't know if they can help. But that's why we're heading east, son. We've got to try."

Billy pulled a pack of Bubble-Yum from his pocket and unwrapped a piece. He had saved this pack, making it last for over six months. Billy knew that it was probably the last pack he'd ever have. The sickly-sweet smell of grape drifted by before he popped it in his mouth.

The second pad required a bit of effort, but eventually settled into place. I leaned over and peeked through the holes in the pads, trying to line them up with the caliper. The gravel bit into my knees.

"Dad?"

I jiggled the first pad a bit, then slid the pins into place.

"Dad?"

"What?" I said, maybe just a touch more gruff than I had intended.

Silence.

I turned and stared into his eyes. His tears reflected the sun. He had a hammer in his right hand and he held it out toward me.

"Can't *you* fix Mom?"

I looked deep into his eyes to see if he understood what he was asking, and then eased the hammer from his hand, feeling the cool, lethal heft of it.

Maybe it would be better for everyone.

The sun set behind us as we made steady progress east. The roads were littered with abandoned automobiles once you hit the rural areas, so the going was slow, but steady.

I looked in the rearview mirror and smiled at Billy. He smiled back.

Absently, as I always did, I reached over and set my hand on Cheryl's leg. She didn't notice, just continued staring at something on the horizon and humming softly.

The time for hard choices was coming, that much was certain.

But not yet.

Not today.

PUBLIC SERVICE

The envelope was five hundred short. It was his first and last mistake.

The punk leaned against the wall, next to the poster advertising some Chinese action flick where a young couple wearing wrap-around shades ran from a couple guys in black suits who were also wearing wrap-around shades. I always wondered why I never saw Chinese movie posters advertising a horror movie. I guess in China, everyone wears sunglasses and no one likes monster movies. Mr. Chang ran a small video stand out of the corner of his restaurant, so he papered the walls in the men's room with posters of all the new releases. He also sold a myriad of touristy junk but his food is the reason the customers came here. As a result, the city forced him to put in a couple of large restrooms to handle the traffic flow. I used the men's room for my meets.

I sat on the edge of the sink with my right hip, and hence my holster, turned away from the punk--Charlie Finkle's his name--and glared at him. "So it's like that, is it?" I said.

I angled my shoulders so that my badge reflected in his eyes.

The automatic air freshener spritzed and the room was flooded with the scent of ammonia and Christmas trees. Someone had bled on the floor near the stalls. So much for the fuckin' janitor.

"I fuckin' ay, *Officer* Schofield."

It was bullshit. If internal affairs even breathed the same air as this punk, the envelope would be empty and not just five hundred short.

This happened sometimes, especially among the guppies.

Okay, I'm not proud of what I do, all right? Police work is a career like any other, and what people fail to realize it that it's probably a bigger rat-race than any mid-level corporate job could hope to be. You get all these guys, most of whom have had little to no formal education and you shove them into a place where up means busts. A good bust can accelerate your career five or six years down the road faster than you can smile for the press.

I used to play it straight.

I walked the clean path for fifteen years. But when you look in the mirror one morning and see all that gray in your hair and realize that you're not one inch closer to a gold badge than the day you walked out of the academy, you begin to examine your options.

You do what you have to do to make those busts, and to make those kind of busts, you need information. You can't use the information that comes out of the department. It's been handled so much that by the time it slithers down to you that the leads are as cold as a Popsicle enema.

So you make your own leads. You corner the small guys, scare the shit out of them, and then you put them to work for you. They pay you a portion of their sales and point you to the bigger fish, and in return, you make sure that they don't get arrested.

It's not as bad as it sounds, you know. Most of the little guys won't sell to kids. The last thing they need is the heat that comes with an eight-year old being found dead with a needle sticking in his arm.

The kids still get the shit, don't get me wrong. I mean, they're born with a carbon-coated silver spoon in their mouth, so they're gonna get it.

But it's not the little guys who give it to them. So, the cop gets a decent living wage for a change, and it gets the real scum off the street. So what if some middle-management types come down slumming to get some coke for their after-hours party? You know what? Some idiot O.D's on junk, it ain't no great loss to the gene pool.

But sometimes your income/information streams start to get cute. It happens. "Fuck you," I say.

Finkle just stared at me, all hard like. It occurred to me that he might have to take a swim in one of the two commodes, or maybe both, in short order. Punks like him have a tendency to forget shit. They forget the reason they started supplying you in the first place.

And well, you know, some of that's my fault. You relax around them a bit to make them more comfortable. When you're a cop you automatically have authoritative body language. They screen you for it in the pre-academy interviews. Certain things will get you disqualified immediately, like talking with your hands. The last thing anyone needs is a cop who's hands are flying all over while he's bitching out a twitchy perp.

As a result, most cops carry themselves like a loaded forty-five.

You can't do that out here. You have to make them comfortable, so you slouch a bit. You let your belt slide down a bit and force your stomach out so that you look like a slob. They're not going to talk to Dick Tracey, you know what I mean? Sometimes they forget, though.

Mr. Chang doesn't really like that I use his restroom for these meetings. Hell, that's just a guess, really. I can't understand more than five or six words outta that guy's mouth. It's all ong and ngyang, you know? The only words I can ever understand are "public service," which he says every time I come walking in his door, his finger pointing toward the men's room.

Don't ask me.

"It ain't gonna fly, Finkle." I said, gripping the cool porcelain of the sink with both hands. "You know and I know it's bullshit, so let's just move it along and cough up the rest of the cash."

He didn't budge. There's a glint in his eye that tells me he's holding a few more cards than he's got on the table and all of a sudden it felt like I swallowed a handful of Mexican jumping beans. I had to think. "Fuck this," I say. "I gotta take a shit. When I come out, we're through playing."

I needed to get to my gun without him seeing it.

The door pushed in on the stalls. I always preferred that. If some dumb schmuck should happen to walk in on you, you could stop the door with your hand before he got it halfway open. I unhooked my belt and pulled it around to the front so I could rest it on my lap while I sat down. The last thing you want is for your weapon to be within reach of whoever happened to be in the next stall and could reach underneath quicker than you could notice. I pulled the envelope out of my pants pocket and recounted. Six hundred dollars. There was supposed to be eleven, but six was enough.

Shit. Shit, shit, shit.

There was just enough to push the extortion charge, a felony. Five hundred and it was simple strong-arm. I was being set up. The cool steel of my Glock felt good against the lifeline of my right hand. That was palmistry I could get behind.

I leaned down and peeked under the wall of the stall. Finkle's boots hadn't moved an inch. The fluorescents glared down with quiet heat and sweat beaded my forehead. I figured I'd better produce while I was sitting here or he'd start to get suspicious. The way my stomach was turning, it wasn't difficult. My fart echoed the confines of the stall.

I sat back up and started folding the c-notes into tight, little balls. I was going to have to swallow them.

Chances are pretty good that Finkle wasn't wearing a wire. It would have gone down already otherwise. I figured if I jerked the door open, I could have him staring down the nine millimeter gates of hell before he pulled. I'd look stupid with my pants around my ankles, but I didn't think he'd be paying much attention to that.

My hand got as far as the door before Finkle moved. I watch his boots walk by in front of me. Next thing I know there's a squeak followed by the click of hard plastic against porcelain and Finkle's taking a crap in the other stall.

For the first time I noticed where some wise-ass left his calling card on the wall. It says, "I fucked my wife's mother and my wife's sister on the same night." Right below it someone had written, "That must have been the night I fucked your wife."

I couldn't help but chuckle, and it didn't hurt matters that I did. Finkle didn't find it funny, though. If this really was a set-up, then the cavalry was late. If he was bluffing, he was screwed.

It happened sometimes. A cop would find out about another cop's source and try to take over the money, and Finkle was just the kind of wimp you could manipulate into something like that. I had to play it safe, though. He could be waiting in there for me with his snub pointing to the door. I needed to make up my mind quick.

That's when the pipes groaned. It caught me by surprise, this being new plumbing and all. I peeked under the adjoining wall just in time to watch Finkle's legs shoot out straight. I heard a sharp intake of breath; then a grunt. I watched as Finkle's legs were yanked back. His boots disappeared from sight and I heard a thump on the wall above my head. Next thing I know, I hear what sounds like a water balloon exploding and blood flew everywhere.

My shoulder slammed against the wall as I jumped. My bare ass smacked against the floor.

I was shitting, but my ass was no longer on the pot.

I scrambled to get to my feet, but kept slipping in the blood, like I was trying to crawl on a treadmill cranked up to its highest speed. I grabbed the door handle and rattled it six or seven times before I remembered that it was locked. I slammed back the bolt and yanked the door back and in and in doing so, caught the edge square between my eyes. It was just enough push to send me flailing backwards. Pain exploded in the back of my head as my skull hit the commode, and that, as they say, was that.

When I came around, my wrist was cuffed to the pipe under the sink. The memory of how I got here came hurling back and my eyes popped open. Two men in identical grey suits stood with their backs to me. The guy on the left was a short, balding black man with patches of white hair on the sides of his head that tufted out like they were frightened to still be there. The other one was wiry and rail thin. Bozo and Slink, Internal Affairs. My heart pounded in my chest.

I reached for my weapon.

Gone.

My head pounded and then my stomach tried to exit out my throat when the memory of how I got here came flooding back. "Get me the fuck outta here!" I said.

The suits turned around, but I didn't care. I yanked with my cuffed hand as hard as I could, trying my best to pull the pipe from the wall. The cuff bit into my flesh but the pipe didn't budge. I just knew that any minute now, something was going to come out of that commode and it wouldn't be good.

They must have thought that I was going crazy, because both of them tackled me and pinned me to the floor. Yeah, big threat me, cuffed to the damned wall and lying on my back.

They might have overreacted.

"Calm the fuck down!" Bozo yelled, and then all the fight went out of me as he twisted my free wrist. I hate that Aikido shit.

"Are you going to stop struggling?"

I couldn't really speak, so I nodded my head. He let go.

I mean, what the fuck, you know? Why in the hell would they cuff me in a bathroom full of blood?

I looked around. The blood was gone.

"Where the fuck is Finkle?" Slink asked. His breath reeked of Binanca.

I didn't answer. What was I going to say?

Bozo slapped my face. "Answer the question."

And then it hit me. They had shit. No Finkle, no witness.

"Tell you what, you take me out of here and I'll tell you anything you want to know."

Slink stared at me. Hard. "Bullshit. Tell me where he is and I'll take you out of here."

I was starting to put this together. They watched Finkle come in here. Then they watched me come in here. They wait what seems an appropriate time for the deal to get done and they bust in guns drawn to find Finkle gone and me lying unconscious on the floor with my pants around my ankles. There's no other exit. They couldn't get the warrant for a wire tap without running the risk of someone loyal to me catching wind of it so they had nothing hard to give the D.A. Not that any of it mattered one iota if we didn't get out of here soon.

"I can sit here all day," said Slink. Bozo got up and turned his back. He walked toward the stalls. Both doors were closed.

"I wouldn't do that," I said.

Bozo and Slink shot each other a glance, a knowing glance if you catch my drift, then Bozo looks right at me and says, "Really? I think I'll take a look anyway."

I shut my eyes.

A creak. Then a splash on the floor as if someone had just vomited. Warm drops of viscous liquid splattered across my face and I heard water splashing, splashing . . . then nothing. My nostrils pinched. I felt like someone had just shoved raw salt into my sinus cavity.

I opened my eyes.

Slink was sitting on the floor beside me in a pool of yellow liquid. Crimson petals floated on its surface. The restroom had been repainted red.

"Would you please," I asked, keeping my voice as level as I could manage, "un-cuff me now?"

Slink sat there. I kicked him. Still, he sat there, unmoving. His jaw hung open. A line of spittle hung from his bottom lip as if his sanity was preparing to rappel from his open, gaping mouth.

"Slink, you asshole! Let's get out of here!"

Slink turned to look at me. The right side of his face was covered with blood. He reached inside his jacket and pulled his gun.

"Whoa, whoa . . . I tried to tell you!" But he wasn't looking at me. Slink got to his feet and walked over to the open stall. He kicked open the lid on the commode and shoved the barrel of his automatic down inside the bowl. My whole body tensed. My knees were more a part of my chest than my legs.

Nothing happened.

Slink stood there, swaying left to right.

Left . . . to right.

Ten seconds. Twenty. Slink stopped swaying. His hands fell to his sides, and he turned around.

Our eyes met. "I guess it had enough shit for one day," I said.

"You little . . ." He raised his pistol at me this time.

The tentacle shot out of the commode and wrapped itself around Slink's head. Porcelain exploded beside my right ear at the same instant his gun fired, the shards lancing my cheek. I jerked away in pain and my shoulder almost came out of its socket when the handcuffs stopped me cold. Slick's legs were sticking up out of the toilet bowl, kicking.

It reminded me of water ballet.

I watched as his legs disappeared, foot by foot, into the commode. His feet vanished below the rim of the bowl bloody water gurgled over the sides. Slowly, a barbed green tentacle slid out from the commode. It stopped when its tip rested in a pool of blood, and I watched with sick fascination as the blood slowly vanished. The tentacle rubbed itself against the walls, leaving clean streaks behind.

Then, slowly, it snaked toward me.

The door to the men's room opened. Mr. Chang walked in, and I could see an "Out of order," sign hanging on the outside of the door. Mr. Chang said something in Chinese, shook his head and pulled a glass vial from his apron pocket. He walked over to the commode, popped the top on the vial, and poured the green contents into the bowl.

I watched as the tentacle slid back into the commode and vanished. Mister Chang closed the lid.

Mr. Chang walked over to where I was chained, reached in his pockets and produced a ring full of keys. He picked out a handcuff key and showed it to me. "Wait here," he said. Then, taking the keys with him, he left the men's room.

Just as I was beginning to have unsavory thoughts about Mr. Chang's sense of humor, the door swung back open and Mr. Chang came in, a bundle of clothes and towels under his arm. He set them on what remained of the sink, leaned over and once again showed me the handcuff key. "My restroom," he said. "My business. You use? You cut me in."

I smiled at him. He was a businessman, after all. "You've got it."

He un-cuffed me and left me alone to change.

I washed up as best I could and changed clothes. With my uniform tucked under my arm, I walked out into the restaurant. Mr. Chang was yelling at a young boy in the kitchen. He looked up, saw me, and pointed at the men's room. "Public service," he said.

Yeah, no shit. I think I'll change my name.

You can call me John Q. Public.

SCRATCH

Sunday, June 23, 1:07 P.M.

The Jeep's headlights cut through the night like a flaming sword. Ike Master's hands quivered with exhaustion as he gripped the sweat-slicked steering wheel tighter with every bump on the narrow dirt road. The needle pushed past fifty and his hastily packed overnight bag bounced freely about the cramped interior. The cut on his chest tingled like mad, and Ike felt the front of his dress-shirt adhering to the moisture of the wound.

It should have stopped bleeding by now.

The Jeep bounced hard and Ike's wedding ring bit into his flesh. He yanked his hand away from the wheel and pushed his ring finger into his mouth until his teeth closed over the gold band. What the hell, he thought. Debbie would be at her attorney's office in the morning anyway.

No. He wouldn't let himself give up just yet. If he could just get to the cabin, maybe, *maybe* he could talk to her and tell her how sorry he was and then--

A hard lurch to the right.

It's going to roll.

Ike released his grip on the wheel and the wheels straightened, the Jeep righted itself and he regained control. Ike wiped the sweat from his forehead with the back of his wrist. "Gotta stay calm," he mumbled. "Only a mile left."

A warm trickle of moisture ran down his chest and onto his ample stomach. *What the hell did that bitch do to me? How did I get . . .*

Saturday, June 22, 6:45 P.M.

. . .here? The affair was supposed to be over. Ike allowed his eyes to follow the sheen of sweat on Petra's bare back down to the round curve of her ass as her cream-in-my-coffee skin reflected in the

candlelight. Well, one last fuck for goodbye's sake had seemed like a good idea, right up to the point where he came.

Ike sat up and held his face in his cupped hands. This shouldn't have happened. When he showed up on Petra's doorstep this evening, he had intended to end it. Clean. Snap. He thought he was over her.

But somehow, he always ended up in her bed. The door would open and the scent of jasmine and rose and earth would wash over him from inside her apartment. Always, *always* she would be dressed in something silk. Or sheer. Or edible. And always, Ike ended up inside her apartment, then inside her.

Afterwards he could never remember why he had allowed himself to be led into it. Afterwards he saw past the candles and the silk and swell of Petra's nipples to the voodoo necklace hanging from the ceiling. Or the huge print of Fuseli's "The Nightmare," hanging on the wall above the bed. Her taste was macabre, and often Ike felt as if he'd just wandered into an ancient, hellish apothecary.

The cool skin of Petra's hand slid onto Ike's shoulder. It wasn't comforting.

"Post-coital regret, hon?"

Ike jerked his shoulder free from her touch, stood up and kicked the discarded clothes on the floor until he found his pants. "I'm done, Petra. This is over."

Her giggle drifted in the air like wind-chimes in a soft breeze.

Ike spun to face her. Petra stood at her dressing table, her back to him. Her eyes met his in the reflection of the mirror. "Sure, Ike," she said. Petra reached down and picked up what looked like a bird's claw. Her eyes met his again and this time, she wore an amused smile.

"I'm serious, Petra. Never again."

The corners of Petra's mouth fell slightly.

"I love my wife."

"Of course you do," Petra said and pulled her waist-length raven hair into a knot.

Ike grabbed his jacket off the floor. He pulled an envelope from the inside pocket. "Here," he said.

Petra spun to face him. "Ooh!" She said, snatching the envelope from his hand. "Money?"

Ike watched as she tore it open. "No," he said. Petra unfolded the piece of paper inside. "It's an eviction notice. You have never paid me rent for this place and I want you out within seven-two hours. After that, you can go fuck--"

Petra's hand shot out and slapped Ike hard across the cheek. The vision in his left eye blurred, clearing slowly. "You think I'm just a little itch you can scratch and then leave? That it?"

Ike looked her in the eye. She was beautiful. He snatched her hair in a fist and jerked.

Petra gasped, the amused look fully gone for the first time since Ike had arrived.

"Look, bitch," Ike said. "Just get out. I don't care what the fuck you do. We're through."

He didn't see Petra's left hand slip to his chest. Ike felt heat, then felt something sharp slide into the flesh just above his solar plexus.

Ike jerked back. His hand tangled in her hair and he took a few strands with him. His skin felt seared . . .burned. Ike pulled his hand away and looked at it.

No blood. Just a scratch.

Petra crossed her arms, and in her hand she held the severed foot of a chicken. The wrinkled, green skin attested to its age. The nails were black.

Ike's hand tightened into a fist. He took a deep breath and forced it to relax. "Seventy-two hours," he said, then spun on his heel and strode to the door.

"Seventy-two?" Petra asked. "I give you twenty-four."

Ike snatched his oxfords off the floor. "What the fuck does-- No. I don't even care. Good-bye Petra. You were a great lay."

"I'll tell your wife," she whispered.

Ike stopped in the doorway.

"I'll tell her that while she's been doped up on her little libido-killers, you've been fucking me." She let the words hang in the air. Then, "Be back here tomorrow night, Ike."

"No," Ike said. "We're through. I'll tell her myself, so save your goddamned quarter. You're going to need it."

Petra laughed softly. "Oh, you'll be back. You have no self--

Sunday, June 23, 1:19 A.M.

Controlling his panic, Ike skidded to a stop in front of the cabin. The Volvo, and hence Debbie, was nowhere to be seen. "Fuck!" Ike slammed his fist into the dashboard and was rewarded with a flash of pain from the cut on his chest.

Now what?

Ike eased the fabric of his shirt away from the wound, and in the dark, the white cotton appeared to be stained black. The fabric peeled from his skin like tissue paper from damp roast beef.

Gingerly, he grabbed his overnight bag from the back seat and double-checked to ensure that the bottle of Johannesburg Riesling he had grabbed from the wine cellar at home hadn't broken. It was Debbie's favorite. Debbie might not be here yet, but she would stop here before she left him for good to raid the safe for money. The bank accounts didn't have her name on them, and she'd need money. He'd just be here waiting for her. It was their special place, after all; their weekend retreat.

Halfway to the front door, Ike heard a twig snap in the distance.

He froze. Who knew what kind of friends Petra had? Ike didn't think he'd been followed, but . . . He shouldn't have stopped. He should have just kept walking. If someone was there, they now knew that he had heard them. Ike took a stuttering half step, then realized it was too late. He had hesitated too long for it to go unnoticed.

Ike bolted toward the cabin. If anyone was coming up behind him, he couldn't hear it over his own footsteps and deep, heaving gasps. He fumbled with his keys, then grabbed the familiar square shape and shoved it in the lock. Within seconds he had the door slammed shut behind him.

Hands on knees, Ike sucked in great breaths of air. The cut on his chest tingled, ice and fire fighting for control.

He eased up next to the blinds beside the front door and slid his finger between two of the slats.

No one was outside.

You spooked yourself, he thought, then looked again. The Jeep was the only sign that anyone had been here in days.

Absently, Ike scratched at his chest. The pain was glorious. His fingers felt a ridge of swollen flesh surrounding the outside of the cut. Ike continued to scratch his chest a full three seconds after he decided to stop, and walked toward the bathroom.

A blinking red light caught his attention from the end table beside the couch. The answering machine winked at him, promising great things. Debbie could have called.

He stabbed the message button with his bloody finger.

"Hi Ike," Petra's voice drifted from the speaker. "It's your little itch. I'll see you before morning. You see, that's all--"

With a jerk, Ike ripped the answering machine from the table and slammed it against the stone hearth of the fireplace. Plastic shards sprayed the hardwood floor.

The tingling in his chest flared with sudden heat, the pain sending him to his knees.

He focused on taking deep breaths, in through the nose and out through the mouth and his nose filled with a salty, yet slightly sweet odor. The pain eased, and Ike tore off his shirt to examine the wound. Surprisingly, it wasn't much more than a swollen scratch.

Hi Ike. It's your little itch.

Doubt was slowly being replaced with the first traces of fear. Intuitively, Ike knew what was coming next. If only he hadn't . . .

Sunday, June 22 8:30 PM

" . . .cheated on you." Ike said.

Across the table, past the silver candlesticks and Austrian crystal wine-glasses, Debbie stared back without expression. Her mouth hung open, filled with a bite of un-masticated food. Her eyes were expressionless.

"But it's over. I swear to God, Debbie, it's over." Ike shook his head and tears formed at the corner of his eyes. "I don't know why I did it. I really don't."

Ike waited as Debbie looked down at her plate while she chewed. She set her knife and fork down gently beside the china plate and lifted her wineglass. "Is it really, Ike?" she asked.

"Oh, yes. I swear to you--"

Debbie's wineglass shattered on the wall behind Ike's head.

"You bastard," Debbie whispered. Her eyes were dull; expressionless. "The medication works, Ike. I'm finally starting to feel like I'm alive again. But you can't wait, can you?"

"Debbie, I--"

"Shut. Up." Debbie hissed. "You've had your turn to talk. Just because my sex drive died for a little while, you had to go and find it somewhere else, huh?"

"I wouldn't call three years a little while, Debbie."

"Fuck you. The medication does that to you."

Ike sighed. "Look, I'm sorry. I really am. I tried, you know? I mean, didn't I go to counseling with you those couple of months?"

Debbie stood up and left the table.

Ike sat at the table and watched her go. It was probably best to give her some time to cool off, anyway. He checked his clothes for glass and finished his meal.

Twenty minutes later, Debbie walked out of the bedroom. She had a suitcase in either hand.

Ike jumped up from the table and rushed over to her. "Hey, wait a minute. Can't we--"

"No," Debbie said.

Ike put his hand on her arm. She stared at his hand with a volcanic intensity.

Slowly, Ike eased his grip and backed away.

"Don't try to find me," Debbie said, and then left.

Well, fuck her! Hound won't run, bitch won't fuck, and she's surprised? Gimme a fuckin' break! Below the anger, Ike could feel a gnawing sensation growing in his stomach. He reached up and scratched his chest, all the while his anger beginning to . . .

Monday, June 23, 1:35 A.M.

Fester.

The scratch on his chest was swelling, white and purple ridges forming on either side while blood oozed from the center. Worse yet, it smelled of rotten cheese.

Ike's stomach knotted. He had disinfected it with peroxide from the first aid kit and taped on a clean bandage, but it continued to burn. The itch was taking on a dull, creeping sensation. Maybe a little more peroxide.

As he walked toward the bathroom, Ike absently reached up and scratched his chest. *God, that feels good.* Closing his eyes with relief, Ike scratched until the itch subsided. When he finished, he opened his eyes and took another step toward the bathroom, then stopped suddenly as his eyes caught sight of his fingertips.

They were drenched with blood. Holding his hand out in front of his face as if it belonged to someone else, Ike bolted for the bathroom. He felt a warm trickle on his stomach.

His stomach heaved. Ike swallowed and bit back the urge, but the relief faded fast. He barely made it to the commode before he puked, his stomach heaving with great spasms. The wound on his chest burned hotter with each contraction, and between the lack of oxygen and the pain of the wound Ike thought he might faint.

Slowly his stomach settled and Ike ripped the blood-soaked bandage from his chest. Infection was setting in. The swelling around the open sore was now three times its original size, bubbling like a blister with pinkish hues. And God, how it itched. He thought it was bad earlier, but it was nothing compared to this.

He had to get help. He grabbed the peroxide bottle from the counter. twisted open the cap and splashed burnt red liquid across his chest. The wound bubbled white and red with tinges of yellow. God, how it *burned* . . .

Ike ripped open another gauze pad and taped it over the mounds of swollen flesh. He dashed to the living room and snatched up his jacket from the back of the couch. He yanked open the front door.

And froze in his tracks.

The hood to the jeep stood open. Wired hung over the sides of the engine compartment like limp vines.

Ike backed into the cabin and slammed shut the door, fumbling with the locks. He took a deep breath and swore as another lance of pain shot through his chest.

The phone rang.

He ran to it and snatched it from its cradle. "Debbie? Debbie you've got to get me help. Someone is--"

"Sorry, hon," came Petra's voice from the earpiece. "This is between me and you."

Ike seethed with anger. "What the fuck did you do to me you little bitch?"

"Now Ike, is that any way to talk to your lover?" Petra giggled. "All you have to do is make it until the morning, Ike. Then my friends will leave you alone and you can go to the hospital."

"Fuck you. I'm calling the police. They'll be out here within an hour."

"Good night, baby," Petra said. "All you have to do is show a little self-control for a change."

The line disconnected. Ike punched in 911.

And waited. Silence. He glanced down at the phone and saw that it was disconnected from the wall.

What the . . .

He grabbed the phone cord and plugged it back into its socket.and returned the receiver to his ear.

Nothing.

Ike fell onto the couch. He leaned his head back on the cushion and closed his eyes. Pain flared through his chest, radiating down to his solar plexus and into his shoulders.

Shit!

There was no place to go. No one to call. He had to sit tight and hope that Debbie showed up and then they could take the Volvo to the hospital.

Ike had no doubt that Petra's friends waited for him outside, but if he could dash to a running car, then maybe he could beat them to the punch and get out of there before they got to him. He just had to make sure that he didn't make his wound worse by scratching any more.

But God, how it itched. The hot tickle inside his fleshed begged him to bury his fingers inside of the wound.

Got to think of something else. Got to get my mind off of it.

Ike grabbed the arm of the couch with his right hand and sat on his left, groaning with agony as he tried to ride out the pain.

I will notnotnotnot scratch. It'll just get worse. It'll be even worse the next time. Gotta let it heal. The pain is just the healing. I will not scratch.

Ike jerked his left hand free from under his ass and dug his fingers into the wound. *Oh, God, yes.* It was better, but it wasn't enough. He pushed in harder, digging his fingers into raw flesh. But still it throbbed and burned and itched and crawled. Ike massaged it with the heel of his hand, just around the outside of the wound at first., but it did no good. When the heel made contact with the swollen ridges of flesh, Ike felt something pop. A tepid warmth spread across his flesh like jelly. Ike looked down. Pus and blood streaked his chest.

Still, the itching continued.

The skin that covered the blisters pulled away with the friction, but Ike kept rubbing. His stomach turned with the disgust of the sight, but the muscles in his arm were caught up in the motion like an old car that continued to putter even after it was turned off.

Exerting his will, Ike stopped scratching. He sat, waiting for the itch to return. When it didn't, he exhaled--he hadn't realized he'd been holding his breath--and allowed his weight to settle back into the couch.

He looked back down. His bare stomach was painted red, as if he were an ancient Scotsman preparing for battle.

If I don't stop this, I'm going to kill myself. And then, with sudden realization, he thought, *That's what she wants me to do. I've got to find something to distract me.*

Ike stood and limped into the kitchen.

He stopped in front of the sink and opened the top drawer and took out a dishtowel then opened the freezer door and removed several ice cube trays. He popped out the frozen cubes and wrapped them up. As soon as the towel reached his chest, the familiar ache returned. Spreading . . .spreading . . .

Ike steeled himself for the onslaught of pain, and when it hit, he sharply inhaled and ground his teeth. The ice wasn't helping. The gnawing pulled at his skin like a thousand mosquito engorging themselves at the same time and he was helpless to stop it.

Absently, he began to rub at it with the towel. Slowly at first, as one might stroke a lovers face; then quicker, with more ferocity. Ike realized what he was doing and dropped the towel, then, unable to stop, Ike dug the heel of his hand back into the scratch. But now, even that didn't seem to go deep enough.

Stop this! Ike pulled his hand away and stood there, shaking and shivering with each flash of burning pain. He held off a good two minutes, sobbing all the while.

His resolve broke.

Ike slammed his chest against the kitchen table, grabbed the table leg for support and pulled the sharp corner into his wound; up and down and up and down.

Still not deep enough. The itch is just below.

Ike pulled away from the table, leaving a piece of himself behind.

He bolted to the sink and began yanking open drawers. Finding the object of his search, Ike removed the shiny silver cheese grater, still spotless from the last time it had been washed. Even through the pain, Ike paused and contemplated the severity of what he was about to do.

But the need for relief was too strong.

Grabbing the cheese grater firmly by the top and bottom, Ike began to rake it up and down his chest. Small gobbets of flesh peeled away, sticking to the backside of the steel. He continued dutifully, ripping and rending the tender skin.

Still not deep enough.

Ike threw the bloody steel down in fury. There had to be something else; something more effective.

There! That's it!

Ike grabbed the bottle of Johannesburg Riesling. He looked at the label for a mere moment before he turned the bottle upside down, grabbing it by the neck.

I'm sorry, Debbie, Ike thought, right as he smashed the bottle against the edge of the counter.

The shards of thick glass gleamed in the amber kitchen light. They were perfect.

Ike scratched.

Multiple Pages on a Monday Morning, from the Scrapbook of Infinite Possibilities

When you're seventeen and full of life, with the edge of the world peeking over the rim of next year, it's easy to be certain that nothing will change. The girls still give you a second look when you walk down the street. The men still talk about you in the barber shop, wondering how many touchdowns you'll throw next year and making five-dollar bets on whether you'll go to state. The tough challenges are just in front of you, they say, but you've got what it takes to make it through. You've got the goods.

You're the next, best thing and the future is wide open. Everything you do is golden; every decision for the best.

And then, as quickly as it started, it's over.

•••

"So, what happened?"

If you've never been kicked in the groin or sucker-punched by a supposed friend, you won't understand the feeling of having your son flip through your high school newspaper clippings and asking that question. In some ways, he's just like me at his age. He's the high school quarterback, he's good at it, and he's something of a smart-ass. Football's a Whytsel family tradition.

So is being a smart-ass.

Barbara, his girlfriend, is sitting on the couch next to him. Her parents own the only fast-food restaurant in town, along with the drive-in theatre and a tenth of the real estate on the east side. She's a cheerleader, and much to my discomfort, she looks a number of years older than Danny, my son, while being the same age. Her hair is mussed in such a way that I know they were making out before I got home.

I used to date a Barbara when I was his age.

"What do you mean, 'What happened?'"

"There's nothing in here from after your junior year."

I walk into the kitchen and pull my pants up over the roll of fat hanging from my stomach. I still remember my mother telling me never to let myself get this big. "It's the most unattractive thing in the world," she'd said, "a man with his stomach hanging over his belt." When she died a couple years back, I didn't cry. I know it's in me, somewhere, just waiting to come out, but it hasn't happened yet.

Barbara mumbles something I can't make out, and I hear Danny say, "Beats me." There's a moment of silence before the giggling starts. There's still some meatloaf left over from yesterday's dinner, so I pull it out the refrigerator. It's the frozen kind, the type you buy pre-made and then throw into the oven for an hour. Something about the paper pan it comes in irritates me. It's like everything else in this house; easy and pre-made and lacking in any taste whatsoever; bachelor style.

"You eat yet?" I call out.

There's a moment of silence, then, "I'm eating at Barbara's tonight."

Nothing new there. He spends more time with her than with me. I guess it's only to be expected. Next year he'll be a senior then before I know it he'll be off to college on a football scholarship and he's starting to resent the fact that he isn't there yet. There's a very selfish part of me that wants him to break up with her, that wants someone else to come along. Then there'd be that "getting to know you," period where they'd still have their separate lives, where they'd still spend time with their other friends instead of waiting for the next opportunity to get their hands down the front of each others' pants. I just hope he's smarter than I was at his age.

"Ten o'clock," I say. "You've got practice tomorrow."

He calls back, "Yeah," and I can tell he has no idea what I just said.

When my food is finished, I go back into the living room.

They're long gone.

●●●

If you have a good front line, the option is one of the most indefensible plays in football.

The quarterback sets up under center, takes the snap and then sprints down the line while the running back trails behind him. Once you get to the end of the line of scrimmage, you come face-to-face with the defensive end. These guys are usually fast and tough, and they love to see the ball coming their way.

At this point, the play derives its name.

The quarterback has to determine if the defensive end is going to tackle him, or if he's going to step up and cover the running back. If he goes for the tackle on you, the quarterback, then you wait for him to make contact and pitch the ball out to the running back, who scampers down the field. If the defensive end waits for you to pitch the ball to the running back, you turn up-field and run it yourself.

You don't see a lot of teams running the option these days. A quarterback has to know the assignment of every player on the team. It's his job to make crucial decisions on the spur of the moment, and as such, the position is one of the most difficult to play and therefore the hardest to fill. The option tends to get the quarterback injured, as he's taking hit after hit after hit.

And it hurts.

If you're running the play correctly, you're getting hurt.

I wasn't anywhere near as fast as our running back, so in order to make the play work, I'd run directly at the defensive end and make him commit to me so that I could pitch the ball.

I'd end up flat on my back with a helmet buried in my stomach, but the crowd would cheer.

Every time I'd feel the pain, the crowd loved me more.

Run correctly, the option is indefensible. But someone has to pay the price.

●●●

Grantston Grinds Concord

Reggie Whytsel, also a drummer for the Grantston County Band, laid down his drumsticks long enough to throw three touchdown passes for a 56-7 victory Friday night against the visiting Concord Blue Waves.

I told myself I wasn't going to do it, but the meatloaf was cold in the middle and there was nothing but reruns on the tube, so I ended up with the scrapbook lying open in my lap, staring at my past.

It was my favorite clip. Barbara was in the picture. Not Danny's Barbara, but my Barbara. The photographer had caught her in mid-jump, her knees bent and her pom-poms stretched toward heaven. Whenever I thought of her, I thought of this picture. It was a better way to remember her than any of the others.

Here she was happy.

I still wonder where she is now, what's she's doing. She was seventeen in the picture. She was pregnant at eighteen, married at nineteen, divorced at twenty, and gone from my life forever at twenty-one. Danny was all I had left of her.

I like to dream that she went on to college, and she finished her degree in Marine Biology and she's working somewhere in the Mediterranean alongside the world's smartest people. Maybe she married one of them and had a family; one she could be proud of. Then again, maybe she's somewhere right now, sitting around in her empty house, staring at eighteen-year old press clippings.

Probably not.

I tell myself over and over again that I won't look at the damned things. I keep meaning to throw the scrapbook away, but I never get around to it. The past was easier to deal with when you didn't have it staring you in the face all of the time. I'd almost forgotten about it until Mom died, and my sister found the scrapbook while cleaning out her apartment. I even told my sister to send it to me, thinking the nostalgia would do me good.

But it's hard to take comfort in the accomplishments of the past. Every time I read one of the articles, I wonder if I'm not reading about the best moments I'll ever have in life, and it's all downhill from here. Then you remember all the mistakes that got you from then to now, and you either fall asleep to bad dreams or wake up to a worse hangover.

Eighteen years ago, the crowds cheered as I led my team to victory.

And I hated it.

So when the season ended, I quit. In a town where more prayers are issued on Friday night under the stadium lights than on Sunday morning, it didn't exactly endear me to anyone. But I'd had enough.

When you're seven and watching Terry Bradshaw throw touchdown after touchdown in the Super Bowl, they don't tell you about the groin pulls that make walking almost unbearable. They don't tell you about the bloody mouth from a linebacker's cheap shot under the pile of bodies after a tackle. They don't tell you about the fingers in the eye, or the separated ribs or the broken noses.

They only show you the power. And the glory. Forever.

Amen.

●●●

Sandy woke me with a shake. "Come to bed," she said.

I'd fallen asleep in my chair. The scrapbook lies open in my lap. I must have been thinking of my mother again. She passed away a couple of years back, and I still miss her. Next to Sandy, she had been my best friend. I still haven't gotten over her death.

I start to close the scrapbook when the clipping catches my eye.

Concord Edges Grantston 27-26

Reggie Whytsel, also a drummer for the Grantston county marching band, laid down his drumsticks long enough to throw for one hundred fifty yards and one touchdown Friday night, but it wasn't enough to overcome the visiting Concord Blue Waves as Grantston dropped its third straight game.

The coach let me play three more games after that before replacing me. I didn't go out for football the next year, and no one cared. Once the pressure to win was gone, my mother and I had spent a lot more time together.

"You remember this?" I ask Sandy.

She's tired, and I can tell she really doesn't want to talk about it, but she comes over and sits on the arm of my chair anyway. Her robe falls open, exposing her flannel pajamas underneath. "Of course I do," she says. "It's the night I got up the nerve to ask you to dance with me."

"We almost won that game," I said. "If I hadn't screwed up with those interceptions, we'd--"

"Isn't that the game where Barbara broke up with you?"

It takes me a minute to remember. "Yeah, I think it was."

Sandy rests her hand on my shoulder. "Then there you go. If you hadn't lost that game, you wouldn't have shown up at the dance with those big, sad puppy-dog eyes, I would have never taken pity on you and we wouldn't be together now."

I look up at her and smile. I do that often, it seems.

"Now close the book and come to bed," she says.

I do.

As I slide under the sheets next to her, I thank God again for Sandy. I couldn't have asked for a better wife, and I tell her that as often as I can.

If only we could have had children.

● ● ●

Once you establish the option as a viable threat, you can build a variety of plays off that foundation. Since the defense has to stretch wide in order to keep the option from being too successful, it opens up counter plays, starting one way then suddenly shifting direction. The defensive backs have to play up tight on the line of scrimmage, giving the receivers an extra step for the long pass. The linebackers have to protect the ends, which leaves the middle open for a good trap.

But if you, the quarterback, aren't willing to sacrifice yourself to establish the option, none of it matters.

You become one dimensional, and at that point, you're no good at anything.

● ● ●

Danny doesn't get in until after one. He wakes me up with a shake. I fell asleep in my chair again. The scrapbook, and the article extolling my high school team's victory, lies open in my lap.

He doesn't wait around for me to wake up enough to remember he's in trouble. By the time I realize how late it is, he's already in his room. I'm angry, but not angry enough to barge in on him. I can always talk to him tomorrow, before school.

Assuming I wake up in time, that is. I don't open the bookstore until eleven, and I've been getting in the habit of sleeping in lately.

He's a good kid. Smart and talented as hell. The scouts are already all over him, and it's just his junior year. He's just going through a phase. I know I did when I was his age. My mother raised me on her own, and at seventeen, she was the last person I wanted to talk to.

That's not true. She was the first person I wanted to talk to, but she wouldn't listen. Whenever I'd try, it would be like talking to a brick wall. I lived in my world, she lived in hers. Try as I might, she couldn't understand me.

She lived in a world of churches and V.F.W. meetings and poppy sales on Veteran's Day. I lived in a world of letter jackets and weight training and championship banners looking down on me from the stadium rafters like ancestors in a Shinto temple.

There wasn't much middle ground there.

But that wasn't the case with Danny and I. I remembered what it was like to be in his position. I was there, in the trenches. I understood his world. He could talk to me.

I just wish he would, is all.

I'll talk to him in the morning.

Right now, I'd much rather just go to sleep. I start up the stairs, but stop two steps up. Think I'll sleep in the chair.

I want to look at my scrapbook some more.

● ● ●

I'm reading the sports page when something strikes the paper.

I pull the paper down and look over the top. Sandy is sitting across from me at the table, her head buried in the new issue of Architectural Digest. A single, drenched square of Frosted Mini-Wheats lays on the table between us. The back of the sports page is streaked with milk.

"You wanted something?" I ask, smiling.

"Hmm?" she asks, her eyes wide with mock innocence.

I fold the paper in half and set it on the table. "If you had something to talk about, all you had to do was ask."

"I didn't want to interrupt you," she said.

"You--"

"But since you're finished reading, what do you think about going into the city this weekend? Catch a show. Stay at the Waldorf. Maybe fool around in the back of a taxi cab on our way back from dinner?"

I give her my best disapproving look. "We're much too old for that kind of nonsense," I say. "They'd never let us into a show."

"Don't tease," she says. "Yes or no?"

"I'm not sure I can get away this weekend," I say. I'm the band director for the high school and it's competition season. We really need the practice. "We've got the Wood Festival next weekend and we really should schedule one more--"

As innocently as possible, Sandy slowly pulls the front of her sweatshirt up and flashes me.

"City sounds good," I finish.

She picks up a piece of toast and turns her attention back to the magazine. "I'll call and get tickets," she says. "Go back to your sports."

I stare at her. She isn't paying attention to me, but she can't quite hide the grin.

It's one of those moments I'll remember forever. Once again, I'm reminded that in spite of all the regret, we couldn't have this life if we had children.

Life was made up of infinite possibilities.

You just couldn't have more than one of them at a time.

● ● ●

The smell of smoke wakes me up. Danny's in the kitchen, pouring himself a glass of milk while his bagel burns. I really have to remember to buy a new toaster. The one we have was old when we bought it at the thrift store.

He doesn't even see me come in. Screaming lyrics emanate from the bud-style earphones stuffed into his ears. I pop up his bagel and open a window, which finally gets his attention.

Danny looks at me, then the toaster and shouts, "Sorry!"

I cross my arms and stare at him. Finally, he turns off the music. "I said I was sorry," he says.

"One o'clock?" I ask.

He turns his back on me. "We were playing cards with Barbara's parents and lost track of time. You can call them if you want."

It's a preemptive offer. He doesn't think I'll do it, so he's offering it up to make his story sound better. Nice trick, but it's one I've used myself. I pick up the phone.

He's good. He completely hides the look of panic that I know rushes through him. "They probably won't answer this early," he said. "They don't usually wake up until noon. You can try them then, if you don't trust me."

Stage two. Invoke mistrust and other negative emotions into the conversation in order to deflect the fact that he's lying.

"Of course I don't trust you," I say. "You're seventeen."

"Right. I'm almost an adult. So cut me some slack."

Stage three. Obfuscate misdeeds in the pending age of majority.

"So act like one," I say. "You've got practice today, and you're not going to be good for anything if you don't get your sleep."

For the first time in ages, I see the look of defiance leave his face. "Yeah, that's true," he says. There is sadness in his eyes I recognize all too well. "Sorry, Dad. It won't happen again." Just when I think we've made some progress, he adds, "On a school night."

I can't help but laugh. "Okay, here's the deal," I say. "You get in at ten on school nights and we'll push your curfew up to one on the weekends. Deal?"

He nods while guzzling his milk. He looks better, but there's still something eating at him.

He wipes his mouth with the back of his shirtsleeve. His brow wrinkles. With a sigh, he asks, "You think we can win State?"

I think about it for a moment, then nod. "Yeah, you can. But it doesn't matter if you don't."

He rolls his eyes. "Right. Easy for you to say."

"You think I don't know what that pressure is like?" I ask. "I was in the exact same boat as you. We were expected to go all the way. It didn't matter if we didn't have the size or the speed. In this town, if you can win, you can win State. It's expected."

"But you didn't, right?"

"Nope. We lost in the first round of the playoffs. I gave it everything I could, but it just wasn't enough. After that, I quit."

Danny stares at me, like I'm something from another planet. "You what?"

"I quit," I say. "I hated football. I hated waking up every morning in pain. I hated having the coach pop my shoulder back into socket at halftime so I could go back out and play. I hated all the old men with their expectations and the fact that no matter how good we were, we still weren't as good as their team, or last year's team. I got tired of it, so I quit. That's why there aren't any clippings from my senior year."

"Why?" he asks. "You were good. You could have gotten a scholarship. You just threw it all away because of the pain?"

I shake my head. "Not just the pain," I say. "There were lots of reasons. Then you came along and I didn't have time for it. Your mother and I had to make a lot of changes in our life to raise you."

Danny crosses his arms. "So it's my fault?"

"That's not what I'm saying at all. It was just one of many reasons--"

I don't get a chance to finish. Danny shakes his head and walks out of the kitchen. I follow him. "I had already made up my mind to--"

"Don't worry, Dad," he says. "I won't make the same mistake."

"You're not listening to me," I say. "You weren't a mis--"

"I wouldn't," he says, tears welling up, "want to end up like you, after all." He's under too much pressure for someone his age and I didn't give him the help he needed. I open my mouth to tell him I'm sorry, and then he's gone, out the front door.

His team wins State. He breaks up with Barbara, and dates three different girls the next year. He gets his scholarship, goes to Penn State and ends up being drafted in the third round by the Dolphins.

By the time he's thirty-three, his career is over, but he's made enough money to never have to work again.

I sent Christmas cards for ten years, and tried to call him, but I stopped when he didn't return either. I saw him on television right after he got married. He looked happier than I'd ever seen him.

Maybe one day we'll be able to work it out. At least he got his chance.

●●●

The lights of Times Square shine in through the windows of our taxi, and traffic has us at a standstill. The driver is going off on something different every twenty seconds. He started with the governor's race and moved on to road construction and now he's talking about his daughter.

That's when I feel Sandy's hand move up my inner thigh. I grab her hand and shoot her an expression of shocked disbelief. She giggles.

The trip had been just what we needed.

"Fine," she says. "You won't let me jump you in the back of the cab, then talk to me."

"About what?" I ask. It's hard to concentrate on anything at all with her perfume filling the cab. I just want to get back to the hotel and ravage her.

"Anything," she says. "Just get my mind out of the gutter for a minute."

I lean forward and ask the driver, "How long you think we've got?"

"Thirty minutes?" he says with a shrug, then continues telling us about his family.

I snatch a fifty out of my wallet and hand it to him over the seat. "Keep it," I say. "We'll walk from here."

Before he can say another word, we're out of the cab and walking arm-in-arm toward our hotel. The noises of Manhattan shriek at us like wild animals from their cages.

"This isn't as romantic as I thought it'd be," Sandy says as we pass by a nightclub patron puking in an alley.

"Ah, the glorious city on the hill," I say, and we quicken our pace. "Good choice, honey."

"Well at least you're not sitting in your chair staring at that damned scrapbook."

"You know, it's funny you should mention that," I say. "I've been thinking a lot about it the last couple of weeks."

"Really?" she says. "I hadn't noticed."

I pull her in tight to my side. "There's my smart ass," I say, smiling. "But it's been bugging me, you know?"

She can tell I'm getting serious now, so she lets me go on.

"It's weird, but I can't get it out of my head. Have you ever thought about the crucial turning points in your life?" I ask. "The spots in time where a single decision ended up changing your entire life?"

Sandy nodded. "All the time," she says. "But not for long. It's really kind of pointless, isn't it?"

"Of course it's pointless," I say, "but that doesn't mean I don't think about it. I think one of those moments was back then, when I was playing football."

"How so?" she asks.

"I remember at the beginning of the year, when we were just learning our plays. We were an option team. It was the first play we worked on in camp and the last play we ran every day. Everything we did was built off it."

"I remember," Sandy says. "If I recall, you weren't the best at running that play."

"Exactly," I say. "But I could have been. I remembered the point where I figured out what it took to make the play work. When I sacrificed my body and made the defensive end tackle me, the play ran great, but it hurt like hell getting pounded like that.

"But once I decided to have fun and not get hurt so much, the play didn't run so well."

"What's your point?" she asks.

"The games we won?" I say. "Were the games where I decided to cope with the pain and run the play as well as I could. Everything else worked like a charm after that. The games where I just wanted to have fun, we lost. And I decided early in the season to just have fun and not worry about it. Had we won every game--had I actually decided that fun was less important--we could have won every game that season. I might have ended up with a scholarship and who knows what my life would be like now."

Sandy snuggles in closer to me. "Maybe," she says, "But don't forget, you win all your games and Barbara doesn't break up with you. We don't get together."

"I know. It's just weird, how one simple decision can change your life so much."

"For the better," Sandy says, resting her head against my shoulder.

"For the better," I agree. But the lingering doubt remains.

We're almost to the hotel when the mugger jumps us. Sandy jerks back on her purse and all I can do is watch as he shoves in the chest with both hands and she falls back, her head catching the corner of the red brick wall. I'm too terrified to even move. Before I can yell, he's got her purse and is gone.

I stare down at the most precious thing in the world while she dies, her life spilling out onto concrete that reeks of Pabst Blue Ribbon and there's no amount of screaming or yelling or crying that can change what's happening. The decisions that placed us here, in this spot, at this moment happened long ago.

And there's no way to change them now.

●●●

I wake up feeling like I've been struck in the chest with a sledgehammer, but then I'm told that's normal after bypass surgery. Too many years of the bachelor lifestyle meant too many years of terrible food and not enough exercise.

The only good thing about the trip to the hospital is seeing Sandy Bright from High School again. She's a nurse here. She's been divorced a couple of times, but she's making it okay on her own. Never had kids, though. I tell her that's a shame.

That's when Danny walks in the room. Even though I have seen him in over a decade, I'd recognize that face anywhere. He looks great, fit. I can tell he wants to smile, but he's worried that I'll be upset with him. "Hey kiddo," I say. "Missed your curfew again, I see."

"Sorry Dad," he says. "Got tied up." He scans all the machines they've got me hooked up to and says, "I'm not too late though, am I?"

I shake my head. "You're here, aren't you?"

"Yeah," he says. "I'm here. Sorry it took so long." Both of us just kind of stare at each other for a while, and then he reaches into the backpack he's got slung over his shoulder and says, "Brought you something from home." He hands me my scrapbook. "I know how much you used to love looking at this."

I hold it in my lap for a minute. Something about it feels strange, wrong somehow, like it doesn't belong here. Then again, the pain medication they have me on is enough to make anything feel strange. "Thank you," I say.

"Aren't you going to look at it?" he asks.

I fumble with the front cover, and my hand begins to shake.

The scrapbook slips from my grasp and falls off the side of the bed, the pages flipping one by one.

Rip thirty-eight, the option to the right side of the line. We break the huddle, up by seven in the second quarter. Hike on two, pads collide, safety is blitzing, turn the corner and the defensive end is there, waiting, ready to deliver the blow . . .fake the pitch, turn upfield, gain three, there's pain but it's not so bad, take it take it take it--too late.

Barbara slips away in the middle of the night. She leaves her wedding ring lying on the bathroom sink. I don't try to find her.

Flip.

. . .turn the corner and he's waiting, breath steaming from his faceplate like an angry bull, pitch the ball, loss of three on the play, no pain, take it take it take it--too late.

Sandy and I take the cab to the hotel and make love all night. Two weeks later, she sees a little boy playing on the curb, getting ready to run into the street. She ignores him, trying not to think about what he'd look like with her eyes and my nose and her protective instinct doesn't kick in fast enough and the boy explodes against the grill of the onrushing car right before her eyes. Three years later she dies of alcohol poisoning.

Flip.

. . .turn the corner, defensive end is waiting, nervous, afraid of screwing up the play we've been running all over him all night long, he's scared of me, terrified, turn right at him and run him over, cleats raking his stomach, gain twelve, here's this life take it take it take it--too late.

I win the playoff game, and every other game in my high school career. I get the scholarship to USC, where I shatter my knee in a scrimmage my sophomore year. I get hooked on vicadin, for the pain, and take five too many before going out surfing in Ventura just after a major storm. The last thing I remember is the sting of salt-water in my sinuses.

Flip.

. . .turn the corner, slip and fall, coach is in my face, not concentrating, not good enough can't I do anydamnedthing right? Where's my pride, whistle blows, back on the field, won't let him down can't let him down, turn the corner, run at the end, take the hit, stand up sucking for air, win the game, don't disappoint, take this life, take it take it--too late.

Danny doesn't play football. He tries out but isn't good enough to make the team, so he quits trying. I push him to at least make the effort if he enjoys the game, but in the end, he hates me for it. That, and for driving Barbara away. Eventually, he tracks her down through the internet and moves in with her. I never see either of them again.

Flip.

Sandy doesn't love me.

Flip.

I clean up my act and never have the heart attack. I never meet Sandy at the hospital. Danny never comes to visit me, and I don't see him again. I live a long life and die in a retirement home, surrounded by others just like me. We all sit and stare at our scrapbooks and make wishes that can't come true.

Flip.

. . .turn the corner, defensive end is waiting, angry, mean, pain waits I hate the pain I hate this game, gotta take the hit don't want to had enough but if I don't if I don't then do it for them do it for this turn into it helmet buries into my ribs and

The scrapbook lands on the floor, closed. My eyes are closed. I'm afraid to open them.

"You okay, Dad?" Danny asks.

I take a deep breath and nod. Slowly, I open my eyes.

Danny retrieves the scrapbook from the floor and places it gently on my lap. "I brought your grandson with me," he says. "But I didn't want him to see you like this. I figured when you get home . . ."

"My grandson? You did?" I ask.

"Maybe you can show him your clippings," Danny says.

I take the scrapbook from my lap and drop it into the trashcan beside my bed. "I don't think so," I say. "There are plenty of other things to talk about."

Danny's eyes widen and he reaches for the book. I stop him with a gentle hand on his arm. "It's okay. I don't need it any more."

"But it's got all your--"

"Let it be," I say. "That's not me in there."

He looks hard into my eyes for a minute, and then nods. The next three hours of sitting and talking with Danny are the best in my life. Eventually, Sandy runs him off when visiting hours are over, but he doesn't go easily.

"We don't have to do it all at once, son," I say. He smiles at me and heads back to the house for the night.

Sandy comes back in a minute later to change my IV. "Good visit?" she asks.

"Long time coming," I say.

"You know," she says, "I had such a crush on you in high school."

I reposition my shoulders to look at her better. "Really?"

She doesn't look at me. "Don't go and get yourself all worked up about it," she says. "Give yourself another heart attack."

And just like that, she's finished and leaves the room. I think I catch her blushing on her way out.

Now that I'm leaning this way, I can see my scrapbook sitting in the garbage can. Thankfully, it's still closed.

●●●

Sandy pulls the blanket tighter around us and slides her hand onto my thigh. The stadium lights blaze, frosting the wisps of fog which creep across the field. Sandy's mumbling something about the abysmal architecture of the high school and I wonder if she's ever going to go back to college and pursue that dream.

I have no idea if she will or not.

Danny gets back from the refreshment stand, hands me my hot chocolate and sits down beside us.

It's the first game of my grandson's football season. He plays wide receiver. They're not very good, but you can tell they're having fun out there, and that's all that matters. Danny winces every time his son takes a hit, but I can see how much he wants to be out there again with the crowd cheering and the band playing and girls screaming his name.

I lean over near his ear and say, "They say you can tell how boring someone's life has been by how far back they have to go for glory."

He shoots me a confused look. I watch his face as realization sets in and with it, a simple grin. He puts his hand on my shoulder and squeezes. "Good point," he says.

"No regrets?" I ask him.

"A few," he says. "Nothing serious. Nothing I'd change if I could."

Sandy leans forward and glares at the two of us. "What are you two chattering about?"

"Guy talk," I say. "Quit being so nosy."

Danny leans away from me, out of the blast radius.

"Oh, okay," Sandy says. Just when I think I'd gotten the better of her for once, she adds, "Nothing important, then."

Danny chuckles. "You ever win against her?" he asks.

I look down onto the field where my grandson's team has fallen behind fourteen points in the first quarter. "Who says I want to?" I ask.

The hot chocolate is too hot and burns my tongue as I take a sip. The blanket doesn't keep me warm enough. Sandy's arthritis flares up about halfway through the second half and we have to leave early. A perfect night it's not.

But I've got to agree with Danny. I wouldn't change it for the world.

I don't keep scrapbooks anymore. Our wedding pictures are still in the envelopes they came in, tucked away neatly in the bedroom closet. I haven't really thought about the past in quite some time.

I guess there'll always be a part of me that wonders "what if?" but I don't pay much attention to that part anymore.

Life may be a book full of infinite possibilities, and no matter what we do, the pages will eventually turn. Thankfully though, I can only read one page at a time.

Ma, Gin and Bug-Eyed Aliens

Don't remember much of the day, now that I try to recollect it. Certain things stick out, mind you, like Ma with that shotgun slung up under her fat old titties or Earl with his coveralls buttoned up on both sides like he was goin' into town for a mixer at Reverend Bob's or somthin'.

And yeah, that flyin' saucer made an impression too, that's for sure.

You know, I would'a probably just napped right through it had it not been for Earl. Hell, we'd all been hearing strange noises for days and tell the truth I'd just grown tired of it. It wasn't nothing really annoying once you got used to it. Sorta like a warblin' sound, like one of them English fire engines on the public television station, but not quite so strong; kinda sick like if you ken my meanin'. I'd just gotten tired of it and figgered it was a buncha dumb kids playin' with a five-n-dime rocket set or a twirly-cone noise-maker or somethin'.

But Earl didn't believe it, I can tell you that. He didn't speak much, but whenever I'd dismiss the noise he'd shake his head and smile at me like he was expectin' something big; like a rich kid come Christmas, you know?

And Ma? Hell, she was pert near convinced that I was makin' the noises my own self so as to go off and investigate with Earl and a bottle of gin.

Not that a soul didn't need a little gin now and then to get past livin' with Ma. I loved her dearly, but that woman could be powerful nasty when she got a mind to it, which was most'n every day, if the truth be told and God be listen'n.

But Earl, now Earl knew something big was happenin' and I'd be lyin' if I didn't admit to a smidgen of trepidation, but when Earl woke'd me up from my rockin' chair that day with his K-Mart slingshot in one hand and a handful of steelies in the other I thought he'd gone on a bender and left me two quarts behind.

But Earl's a big boy, you see. And well, I never did grow much past being able to get my feet to touch the outhouse floor while I was doin' my business so I just played along with him.

My mistake was goin' inside for my flannel.

I just about had my second arm slipped through when Ma walked in on me, that big ol' Gallopin' Gourmet apron running down the front of her body like a fancy, four-foot necktie.

"Where'n you think you're goin'?" She asked. From the look on her face I knew I'd better make it good.

"Well woman, " I said, "if it's any concern of yours, old Earl thinks he saw something fall outta the sky out past the old silver mine."

Her eyebrows raised like two caterpillars trying to escape the sweat pourin' down her forehead. "Outta the sky?"

I prepared myself for an ass whoopin'.

"You know, I heard about those things on the radio," she said. "Art Bell talks about 'em all the time."

I think my mouth hung open at this point.

"I'm goin' with ya'll," she said and started untying her apron.

"Oh, uh-uh woman," I said. "Might be dangerous." I didn't believe anything of the sort, mind you, I was just lookin' forward to a little time away from house with a quart of Earl's best homemade gin and if Ma came along, this would just turn into a long walk for no good reason. "You'd better stay--"

Ma ended that argument like she ended most of them. It's amazing how the sound of twin-barrels being fed with buckshot will pretty much convince a soul of anything.

Earl gave me this look when we got out on the porch, but it didn't take him long to catch the fire in Ma's eye. We decided to leave the old Ford and hike on out the mile, mile and a half to the old mine so as not to scare anything away. Hell, if nothin' else we might be able to scrounge up some rabbit or somethin' so the trip wouldn't be a complete waste.

Well, the sun was going down and the mine was to the west so our eyes got filled with that late evenin' Kentucky sunset. I was enjoyin' it really. Nothing quite like that big old ball of orange fire goin' down over the treeline that really puts one in a drinkin' kinda mood. Earl and me fell behind Ma a little bit and passed his flask back and forth. I took a long pull and like always when you was drinkin' Earl's finest, you had to do your damned best not to cough the stuff right back up.

So I was a little occupied, mind you, when the flyin' saucer buzzed outta nowhere and hovered directly above us.

I gotta say, there wasn't nothing special about it, beyond it violatin' every natural law that I knew of. It looked like any of them flyin' saucers you'd see on teevee or at the movies. It was big and silver and lit up with all sorts of different colored lights and all-in-all it looked like one of them aloo-min-ee-um Christmas trees you see in rich folks homes.

Well Ma had the good sense not to start shootin' at it right away, and Earl just stared up with his mouth hung open like a butterfly net or something. We was all a little disconcerted is the best way to put it, I guess.

I mean, when you're facing overwhelming odds like that, you just be still and hope they don't notice you.

Well, turns out there weren't much hope for that, as outta nowhere five of these little grey men just appears in front of us. They had them funny oversized heads and they were skinnier than a Nashville whore, but Billy Barty sized; short-like.

They looked right into our eyes, and my vision blurred slightly, like as if I was staring through waves of heat off the desert floor. I blinked a couple of times and cleared my head. "Whaddayall want?" I asked.

Them little fellas stepped back, like they was surprised or something. One of 'em pointed his finger at me and everything went all wavy again.

I blinked a couple of times and everything cleared up. "Now you fellas need to stop that," I said. "How do you expect us to hold a civilized conversation if you keep doin' stuff like that?"

I think they were surprised. They kept looking at each other and seemed as if they were all-of-a-sudden as scared of us as we were of them.

That's when I noticed Ma drop the shotgun and start lumberin' all Frankenstein like toward them little fellas. Earl and I just looked at each other in disbelief. Ma didn't take to strangers generally as a rule, but it looked like she wasn't in full control of her senses.

I guess Earl and my brain was too messed up on gin already for them little fellas to take control of us. Well, as much as I complain about Ma, I do love her in my own way and I wasn't letting no little pecker-less gray aliens have their way with her. I jumped in front of Ma and crossed my arms. "Uh-uh," I said. "You just leave'n her alone, now. We don't want no trouble with you guys. If you need to use a phone, there's one over by the freeway Texaco station and--"

Either she comes with us or you do. One of them fellas said. I didn't see his pouty little mouth move or nothin', but I heard it all the same.

Well, when push comes to shove I'm not much of a pusher or a shover. One of them little fellas had what looked like a gun or somethin' in his hand. "Well allrighty then, fellas," I said. "Just bring her back when you're done!"

And then they was gone. Them little fellas, the ship and Ma.

Just gone, like that.

And just as quickly they was back.

They was shovin' Ma away like they didn't want nothin' to do with her all-of-a-sudden like, and Ma was weepin'. That's not something I was used to, that's for sure. Ma kept trying to grab onto one of them little fellas, saying stuff like, "No, don't leave me here! Take me with you!"

But them little fellas wasn't having nothin' doing. They was quick little fuckers, I'll tell you that. Everytime Ma reached out for one of 'em, it was like them big old eyes of theirs doubled in size again. They got their distance from Ma and then they up and vanished again.

Ma was all crumpled up on the ground and a'cryin' like a little baby. When she finally got hold of herself, she said, "They done things to me."

I felt a little horror at that in the pit of my stomach. Poor Ma, I thought. What did those nasty little fellas do--

"And I liked it," she said. "A lot." There was this far off, dreamy look in her eyes that I had never seen before.

Well, we finally got Ma to pull herself together enough to get home. But she ain't never been quite the same since. She bought herself one of them Ham radio sets and taught herself that code thingee and she sits around half the night broadcasting to them aliens to come pick her back up.

The other half of the night, she'd climb up on the roof and lie there naked, waiting.

So I'm guessing there's a moral in here somewhere. You gotta look at things the best you can when they come along and try to learn whatever there is to learn.

I think I've broken it down to two important things:

One, homemade Gin may be what saves us from the impending alien invasion.

Two? Well, I guess that'd have to be that there are certain things that can scare even an advanced society.

Don't think we'll be having too many more problems with them aliens, though.

In spite of what Ma might want.

CC&R'S AT THE WIDDERSHINS PARALLELIUM

"I'm sorry, but I've been very patient, Mr. Petrie. You simply have to do something about the rituals going on in 56703211c. I've washed the bloodstains from my wall four times this week and I simply won't tolerate this kind of thing again . . ."

Shrew. Hag. Fussbudget. Busybody.

None of them properly expressed the entirety of Mrs. Calvetti's nature, but combined they came close. It was all Donald Petrie--wizard, entrepreneur, sophisticate, ladies-man, social-climber--could do to keep from summoning a battalion of wild homonculi to tear the old biddy to pieces.

It wasn't worth disenchantment, however.

" . . .won't strengthen the borders, I'm afraid you're simply going to have to put an end to certain liberties allowed by some of the residents. You can update the CC&R's if you need--we would have done this already if we could form our own independent owner's association--but most of us here, Mr. Petrie, are good residents. We don't complain, do we?"

Donald opened his mouth to answer.

"Of course we don't. We're just trying to do the best we can in . . . ahem . . . unfortunate circumstances. I'm certain you're planning on massive improvements, but if you'll just listen to some of my suggestions I'm positive I can make things easier for you. Now first we simply must do something about the mortgages. They're leaving droppings all over the ether and . . ."

Had it only been two weeks ago? Fourteen days--not the fourteen months it felt like--but only fourteen days had passed since Donald sat in his Park Avenue office, closing escrow with a pair of new residents. Donald rolled an unlit cigar between his fingers and leaned back in his Italian leather chair. The couple on the other side of the desk--Tom and Irene Barker--were perfect candidates, both poor and desperate. Tom had been laid off his job of twenty years after his company outsourced his position to the third circle of hell, and Irene . . .well, Irene was simply a moron.

"I'm still not sure I understand, Mr. Petrie," Tom said. "Don't get me wrong, the price is right, but I don't understand how I can own a house for only two hundred dollars a month."

Irene glared at Tom. Her leg moved slightly and Tom grimaced. "It doesn't matter," she said. "Just sign the papers and be done with it."

Donald smiled wide and looked into Irene's eyes. "Now now, Irene. Your husband is just trying to protect his lovely bride. I have no problem explaining it again."

Irene blushed.

"The truth is, Mr. Barker, you don't own the house. Have you ever heard of the Horizontal Regimes Act?"

They both stared at Donald, mouths open. Donald expected strands of drool to stretch from their bottom lips and watch as the few brain cells the Barkers possessed rappelled down them.

Donald shrugged his shoulders. "It's just a fancy lawyer's term for the regulations defining a condominium." The Barkers seemed to understand, but who could tell? "You see, you don't really own the building. The building itself is owned by the entirety of the tenants. What you technically own is the volume of space within the walls."

Tom crossed his arms. "You mean we're buying air?"

Donald threw back his head and laughed, but he wanted to reach across the desk and smack the idiot. He allowed no trace of the impulse to reach his face, however. You didn't make the kind of money Donald had made in the last ten years by insulting your, "clients.". Well, not while they were around, anyway.

"You're very perceptive, Tom. Were you buying a traditional condominium, that would be true."

"But this is different," Irene said. "It's magic."

"Absolutely right," Donald said. He reached across the desk and flipped open the lid of a mahogany box containing orgasm-inducing chocolates. Irene snatched one up, popped it in her mouth and deflated in her chair with a soft grunt. "You own a portion of a parallel plane of existence. It's a completely different thing all together."

Tom crossed his arms. "I'm not certain I see the difference."

"For one thing, you'll never know you have neighbors. Unlike a condominium, there are no hallways or common areas. We start with a traditional home, then overlap your pocket of alternate reality within the confines. As the actual mass of such a planar structure in the physical universe is almost non-existent, an unlimited number of such parallelium units can co-exist alongside one another without the residents being aware of them at all."

Tom looked ready to drool again.

"It's actually quite easy," Donald said. "You have an enchanted key--" Donald removed a filigreed skeleton key from his desk drawer and dangled it in the air. "--and when you put it in the front door, it triggers a portal to your unit. In every respect, it's exactly like a traditional home."

Irene watched the key rock back and forth, as if being hypnotized.

Tom grimaced. "It's just, well, no offense sir, but I've always found that if something were too good to be true, it usually was. I don't understand why it's so cheap."

"When I can place so many worthy families into one structure," Donald said, doing everything in his power to keep from getting ill, "it's easy to pass the savings along. Most of my money comes from spell component speculation, Mr. Barker, but I was raised poor. I worked my way up from nothing and found that giving something back to the community meant more to me than profiteering from this particular venture." None of it was true, of course. Donald had been born a millionaire and used the skyrocketing real estate costs to turn his paltry millions into some real money.

"Aww," Irene said. "That's so sweet."

"What about the essence clause?" Tom asked.

"It's a minor thing," Donald said, choosing his words carefully. He'd learned that if a deal was going to fall through, it usually happened over this. "It's a magical mortgage."

"A what?"

"A magical contract. It deals with the maintenance fees."

"How much are those?"

"Oh, it's not money. Okay, look. Condominium owners pay a certain fee every month into a common pool for the upkeep of the building and a legal fund, in case of an injury or other unforeseen incident in the common areas. This is the same thing, only with this unit, the upkeep is magical. Without a certain . . .er, refreshment of the spells that keep your unit attached, the barriers between pocket universes can break down. This is a means to keep your home in tip-top shape."

Tom fidgeted in his chair. Irene grabbed for another piece of chocolate. "But it doesn't cost anything?"

"Not one cent. Everyone produces a little bit of magical energy, even those that do not know how to use it. The magical mortgage is a way for you to contribute to a group pool for upkeep of your reality."

"Can't you just do that yourself?"

"I could, but then I'd be spending all my energy keeping up these units when, really, it's your home."

"Does it, um, hurt?"

Donald chuckled. "No, not at all. Your mortgage can take on any shape you want. Dog, cat, bird, we've even got a couple tenants that have fairies. At night, while you're sleeping, your mortgage slips into bed with you and draws the magic out of you and sends it to the group pool. It's as painful as having a kitten curl up at your feet at night."

"I like kitties," Irene said.

"And it doesn't cost me anything? Will I notice it?"

"Do you notice the magic you generate now?"

"Well, no, but . . ."

Donald leaned forward and nodded his head. "It's a little hard to get used to the idea. I understand. I don't want you to do anything that makes you uncomfortable, and this obviously does. Let's just call the deal off. You can find a traditional home and go there. I'm sorry I wasted your--"

"No," Tom said. "It's just . . . okay. Where do I sign?"

With a flick of his wrist, a pen appeared in Donald's hand. "Page seven. And I need your initials here, here, over there, on top of this page, on the back of this one, and--"

And then Donald couldn't move. Bands of bright blue light pinned his arms to his sides.

A voice from nowhere filled the room.

"DONALD PETRIE YOU HAVE BEEN CHARGED WITH TWO THOUSAND ONE HUNDRED AND FOURTEEN VIOLATIONS OF THE MAGICAL ETHICS STATUTES OF THE COVENENT OF WIZARDS, AND TWO COUNTS OF JAYWALKING ACROSS THE STREET IN FRONT OF YOUR BUILDING WHILE GETTING LUNCH AT THE FLESH-LOVERS DELI, YOU KNOW, THE ONE WITH REALLY TART PASTRAMI YOU LIKE SO MUCH . . . ER, ANYWAY, YOU ARE HEREBY UNDER APPREHENSION UNTIL SUCH TIME AS A REVIEW BOARD CAN BE ASSEMBLED TO HEAR YOUR CASE. HAVE A NICE DAY."

If Tom and Irene had vanished any quicker, they'd have been wizards themselves.

"Slum lord," they called him. "Despicable, abusive, syphillistic afterbirth of a wild Centaurian gang-rape." One of the judges had even called him greedy, of all things. In the end, he'd been sentenced to live for a year and a day as a tenant in the Widdershins Parallelium.

That part wasn't so bad, but they couldn't leave well enough alone.

"And," the judge handing down the sentence had said, "no magic other than that necessary to improve the living conditions within the structure."

Okay, well, maybe he hadn't used all of the collected magical energies for upkeep of the building. Maybe he'd used just enough to keep the pocket universes from collapsing entirely. Maybe he didn't return phone calls from angry tenants. But really, you know, it was business. It wasn't like his tenants were paying current market value for a place to live or anything. What did they want for two hundred dollars a month? The more Donald thought about it, the more unreasonable his punishment seemed.

A puff of smoke filled the corner of the living room, followed immediately by the smell of rotten eggs, mold and Chanel No. 5. Donald retched. A small monkey-sized creature with five arms, three legs, multiple sexual organs and purple, matted, permed hair stared him in the eye. "Miss me?" the creature said.

"Yes, but I'll take better aim next time." The council hadn't even let him choose the shape of his magical mortgage. It was simply barbaric.

The creature scamperthumpcartwheeled across the floor and climbed on his back, wrapping one leg around his chest, another over his left shoulder and shoving the third down the back of his pants.

"Hey!

"Homophobe," the creature said. "Get over yourself. It's easier to stay on this way."

"Well then get off!"

"That the best choice of words with something tickling your rump?"

Donald bellowed, felt a tickle in his throat that devolved into a coughing fit. He swung his fists over his shoulders, missing the creature by six inches each time.

"Oooo, mighty hunter. Now quit working yourself into a lather and let's get busy."

Donald bent forward, his hands on his knees. Between gasps for air he said, "Busy . . .doing . . .what?"

"You really want to spend a year and a day in here?"

"Not . . .much . . . .choice."

"Of course there's a choice! The council has instructed me to inform you that they would consider a reduction in your sentence if you made certain necessary improvements."

"Really?" Donald asked.

"Nah, I'm just messin' with you. You're screwed." The creature smacked him upside the head with a free hand. "Get a clue, bright boy! They don't want you in here any more than *you* want you in here. It's bad for business. Who's going to trust a wizard again if word gets out about this? If, on the other hand, you were to make amends, you could just be written off as one bad egg that was effectively dealt with by the council. It makes others more likely to engage in magical business if they know that there's effective recourse in case they end up dealing with . . .well, with assholes like you."

"Thanks," Donald said, shaking his head. "That makes me feel so much better."

"That's what I'm here for. Consider me your own little morale booster. You know, 'Rah Rah Go Team,' that sort of thing."

"I was being sarcastic."

"I wasn't. I'm improving your morale, no?"

"By insulting, smacking, clawing and goosing me?"

"Yeah, but you really want to get rid of me, don't you?"

"Yes!"

"Willing to do almost anything?"

"Yes!"

The creature kissed him on the cheek. "Then I'm doing my job. Look, a Hallmark moment. You had me at 'sarcastic.'"

"You do anything other than watch television?"

"Are you kidding? Hell's been in charge of popular entertainment for the last fifty years! We get to torture and corrupt you all at the same time!"

Donald fumed. "Are all mortgages as annoying as you?"

"Heh. Only the good ones."

There really wasn't anything Donald could do. As much as he hated to admit it, the creature had a point. It might take up all the manna he'd saved over the last few years, and put him in debt for a few more, but it seemed there was only one shot at getting out of this place early.

"Okay, fine. What do I need to do?"

"Well, you could start with the plumbing. There's this small problem with the--"

AAAARRRRRHHHHHHHGGGRRRRSCHNUFF!

Donald jerked as the sound of the scream echoed through the unit. "What the hell was that?"

"Either the shower pipes got cross connected with the lava-pits of Hades again, or Mr. Barnstable in 21663z finally had it with Mrs. Barnstable's cow-tongue casserole. Duck.".

"What?" Donald asked, just before a See-and-Say struck him over the left eye.

"Er, um, I said, 'duck.' The barriers between the planes are somewhat of an issue with the residents as well."

Blood trickled into Donald's eye. The toy--now shattered--spasmed on the floor, the plastic arrow spinning round like a broken compass and announced, "The dog goes, 'Moooooo'."

Donald bolted to the restroom, snatched a washcloth from the rack beside the sink and held it to his head.

The commode--lid closed--gurgled twice, then belched.

"What the . . .?"

It groaned, the tone pitching up and down for a full five seconds. Donald grabbed the lid.

"Not a good idea," the creature said.

It blurped, like thick chili on a hot stove. Donald thought he heard murmuring. He removed his hand from the lid. "That's quite enough of that," he said and prepared a spell.

"Oh no," the creature said and jumped from his back.

Before he could finish the incantation, the lid flew open, a long red appendage whipped out of the bowl and smacked him in the chest. His feet lifted from the ground, the back of his head connected with the shower wall and he slid down, ending sprawled in the bathtub, his feet dangling over the sides. The head of a dragon, fouled with seventeen substances Donald didn't want to identify, snaked its way out of the commode. Dozens of needle-sharp teeth glistened with blood. Hunks of flesh were lodged between them. The dragon's eyes focused on Donald, then narrowed to slits.

Donald held his breath.

A pair of bifocals appeared in front of the dragon's eyes, and it held up a document in front of its snout. "Ahem," it said. "Paragraph forty-three, sub-section two: No modifications will be made to the existing infrastructure of the unit without consent of a super-majority of the tenants and the developer's permission, in writing, filed with the county and Magical Control Board no later than three working days prior to the commencement of spellcraft."

And with that, the dragon slid back into the commode and vanished.

"What the hell was that?"

The mortgage scatterwallopped to the side of the tub and leaned over the edge. "CC&R's," it said. "You know: Covenants, Conditions and Restrictions. You wrote them, after all."

Donald shook his head, which just made the throbbing worse. "No I didn't. My lawyers did."

"More's the pity," the creature said. "Now you're really screwed."

"How am I supposed to fix this place if the CC&R's won't let me do it?"

The mortgage cocked his head and stuck out his bottom lip. "Does somebody need a hug?"

"This is serious!" Donald said.

"Okay, let's take stock: You can't use magic except to fix the building, but you can't fix the building without getting lashed across the room. I guess the only option is to comply with the requirements."

"What? How am I supposed to get thousands of residents to vote on it within a hundred years let alone one if I can't use magic?"

"Well, I can take care of that for you."

Donald blinked. "You can?"

"I'll just take a message to the magic pool where we deposit our collections and have the mortgages take the proposition to the tenants.

You'll have the vote within a couple of days. We can be quite persuasive you know."

"No shit," Donald said. "Okay, fine. Do it."

The mortgage stroked the side of Donald's cheek. "Miss me, my darling."

"GET OUT!"

And with a puff of smoke, the creature vanished.

Two days later, when the mortgage reappeared, Donald lay buried on the couch beneath two blankets, three pillows, four television trays and a rabbit's foot. He wore a stainless steel kitchen pot over his head.

The creature let out a long whistle. "Rough time?"

Donald's voice echoed from within the pot. "Don't ask."

"Okay, here's the skinny: You're screwed."

"What?"

"You don't have a majority yet."

"You're kidding? You mean people actually voted against making improvements?"

The creature chuckled. "Yeah, go figure. Some of them said that they'd rather live like this for another year than do anything that might reduce your sentence. You're not Mr. Popularity around here you know."

"Thanks," Donald said. He removed the pot from his head.

"Others liked things just how they were. They get a certain enjoyment out of the chaos."

"Enjoyment?"

"Yeah, one guy even made us convince him that all the crazy shit that happens here was real. It took three hours to convince him, and then he muttered something about overpaying his dealer. He voted, 'No.'"

Donald stared at the creature.

The creature stared back.

"So what's the final tally?" Donald asked.

"About sixty five to thirty five , in your favor. But some of the residents haven't voted yet."

"Why not?"

"They want to talk to you first. A "sit-down," as the Mafioso call it."

"Really?" Donald said, brightening considerably. "Negotiations I can handle. How many of them do I have to convince?"

"Seventy-three."

"Out of?"

"Two hundred."

A wide grin stretched across Donald's face. "Piece of cake. Let's get started."

One hundred and ninety-nine sit-downs, a black eye, several dozen effusive apologies and a bad case of dysentery from Mrs. Barnstable's cow tongue casserole later, Donald had only talked his way into seventy-two votes. He couldn't believe how unreasonable they were being. Some wanted a percentage of profits, the others simply wanted to insult him to his face. It had taken every ounce of self-control to keep from teleporting each one into a cage full of ex-lax eating monkeys.

"One left," Donald said. "What's this one's story?"

Donald didn't expect it, but there it was. The mortgage actually looked terrified. "Mrs. Calvetti," it said, and then hid under the sofa.

" . . .and we simply can't live like this, Mr. Petrie. You're a terrible, terrible man and your mother would be ashamed if she saw you now I mean the mere chutzpah of even asking us to cooperate after you've done nothing but ignore us for years have you been eating you look peaked you can't not eat, Mr. Petrie, not that anyone would mind if you died of malnutrition--"

Donald's face warmed. "Mrs. Calvetti, I just--"

"--and then there's the matter of the building's appearance just because the inside is made of magic doesn't mean that the outside can forgo some new paint does it Mr. Petrie?"

Donald flexed his fingers. "I--"

"No, it doesn't I've been talking to the other tenants and I know that they're not happy either we don't want the property values to go down now do we? The sidewalk is in desperate need of repairs and oh yes the laundry room don't let me forget to tell you about the laundry room it's quite abysmal the agitator is spitting into your face whenever you open the lid and--"

Donald's stomach knotted in anger. "I intend to do--"

"--would you stop interrupting me, young man you're really quite rude if you can't spend five minutes listening to the concerns of a resident how do you ever expect to be able to fulfill your obligations. And Mr. Petrie?"

"Yes," Donald said.

"The CC&R's?"

"Uh-huh?"

"They're not just obscene."

"Mrs. Calvetti, I--"

"They're not just excessive."

"No, Mrs. Calvetti. Don't do it. I beg you--"

"They're not just monstrous."

"Mrs. Calvetti, I'm warning you!"

"They're downright draconian!"

Donald whipped his hands toward Mrs. Calvetti's face. She flinched, said, "eep!" and exploded like a water balloon full of cherry juice. Blood splattered against the floor, walls, couch, Donald's face, and the face of fifteen tenants in adjacent units.

The mortgage peeked its head out from under the couch. "Oh no," it said.

"I know, I know!" Donald yelled. "I'm screwed!"

A blinding light filled Donald's eyes. When his eyes cleared, the judge who'd sentenced Donald stood before him.

The rush of adrenaline brought on by anger faded. Now he'd be disenchanted. Everything important to him would now be taken away. He'd be normal, just like the marks he suckered every day. But there was nothing he could do. "Go ahead, get to it," Donald said.

"Get to what?" the judge said.

"Disenchanting me. It's why you're here."

The judge smiled. "Quite the contrary."

Donald shook his head. "What do you mean? You said no magic."

"No, I said no magic other than that necessary to improve the living conditions within the building. I don't think one could argue that Mrs. Calvetti's demise was anything but an improvement."

"I get to keep my magic?" Donald said, dumbfounded.

"Not only that, but Mrs. Calvetti's death brings the total number of residents down in your favor. You have your votes."

"I . . . I . . ."

The judge placed a hand on his shoulder. "You can now finish the restoration."

The enormity of the task brought Donald back to reality. "Okay, but it's going to cost me every bit of magical reserve I have. It's still not a win."

"Well, yes and no."

"What do you mean?"

"Other parallelium owners have already heard about your particular acumen in the area of building improvement. There's already three job offers waiting from you from developers. They're willing to pay one million each plus twenty percent of the accumulated magic pool for your assistance." The judge grimaced. "No one wants to become another you, after all."

Slowly, ever so slowly, a smile grew on Donald's face. He felt a warm sensation in the pit of his stomach, quite unfamiliar to him.

"But," the judge added, "your mortgage goes with you on all jobs. We'll take a tenth of your earnings for taxes. You can't just go scot-free after all. That would set a terrible precedent."

"Well," Donald said. "I'm starting to get used to the little beast."

"Somebody does need a hug," the creature said, and crawled up his back.

And with that, the judge *poofed* away as quickly as he'd come.

Donald sighed, collapsed onto a chair, and then it hit him. The warm feeling in his stomach? It was no wonder he'd couldn't identify it.

He'd never felt it before.

It was job satisfaction.

ON THE NIGHTSIDE OF THE ANCIENT, WALNUT MOON

Just past the whorehouse with the invisible walls, through the intersection of Was and Is, Johnny's Pub and Pet Hospital sat nestled between two abandoned buildings which were, in every fashion, identical to the home in which Des Morris grew up. A Wyvern was hitched from the post in front of the Pub, right next to an eagle the size of small elephant.

Des smacked the road-dust from his Levi's and pulled a cigarette from the inside pocket of his burnt-orange leather vest. A crusted-cream hued mutt sat at his feet. The dog looked at Des' weathered face and whined.

"It's okay, Tween," Des said. "We're almost there." The growth just above Tween's hind-leg was bigger than the day before, and the smell was far worse, that much was certain. It had started out as just a slight discoloration on his hair, a dirt brown patch that Des didn't pay much attention to at first. It wasn't until Tween started to favor his left leg over his right that the seriousness of the matter set in. Over the course of days and weeks and finally a month, the discoloration grew into a puffy, fungal, umber-tinted sore that stank of ammonia and rotted meat.

They'd been in the high country hunting the Questing Beast when the disease first appeared. Civilization had been a good hike away--more so because of the slow pace necessitated by Tween's wound--but they'd made it. They were out of food and water.

The tavern offered an end to the suffering for both of their them.

"C'mon, boy," Des said, lighting his cigarette with his last match. Tween limped once, whined, and hobbled on.

Des pushed open the swinging doors to the tavern and stepped inside. The tables were crowded with other Questors. Some wore full suits of armor. Others wore flight suits. All of them were armed. Cigar and cigarette smoke filled the air with a deep blue haze. The air stank of spilled beer and tobacco spit. In the back corner, a jukebox blared John Cougar Mellencamp while a man in a baseball uniform argued with someone in a safari hat over a stack of silver pieces sitting on the pinball machine. Behind the bar, Johnny served up shots of whisky, occasionally wiping his hands on the blue surgical gown he always wore.

Des looked down at Tween sitting near his boot heel. He took another step and Johnny looked up from behind the bar.

The smile of recognition dropped from Johnny's face when he noticed Tween following behind. "Hey, sorry Des. You've got to leave the dog outside. New town ordinance."

"He needs help," Des said. "This is still an animal hospital, isn't it?"

"Yeah, of course," Johnny said. "We're just not allowed to have animals inside, is all. Leave him outside. I'll come out and take a look in a minute."

Had it been any other man, Des might have argued. But he and Johnny went back too far for anything like that. Des knew him from the other world, although from where exactly he never could remember. But that wasn't important. What was important was that he was a trusted friend, and if he said he'd be there in a minute, you might as well write it in stone. Johnny was the best prep guy in the business. It didn't matter what you were looking for, Johnny had the supplies you needed. Add to that the best brew and animal care anywhere to be found and you never really needed to go anywhere else.

Des snapped his fingers at Tween and then backed out of the tavern.

Johnny joined them a moment later. He scratched Tween behind the ears--for which Tween thanked him with hopeful unblinking eyes--then eased him onto his side. Johnny's examination lasted only a minute. "It's the Creep, Des. Too far gone for me to help. I'm afraid there's nothing can be done."

Des' heart sank. "You sure, Johnny?" he asked. "I mean, can't you operate?"

"Well yeah, I could," Johnny said. "But I won't. Fact is, you knew this was comin'. Man brings a dog over here with him, and he can pretty much guarantee it's gonna end badly. Hell, I've got a whole pen-full of the beasts out back that others gave up before the Creep set in. You knew the dangers."

Des sighed and slouched down on the floorboards beside them. He put his hand on Tween's back and looked into the dog's eyes.

It was true. Everyone warned him that this could happen if he didn't let go of the animal, but Tween was a friend that no one else could ever match. He'd been there when Des was sick. He'd been there when the world threw problems at him that he simply couldn't muster the courage to face. He'd been Des' best friend and asked nothing in return. Des wasn't going to abandon him now.

Des glanced up at Johnny. Their eyes met and Des leaned in close, so as not to be overheard. "What about the Citadel?" he asked.

Johnny stiffened. His brow furrowed and his bottom lip began to twitch. "You gonna ask me about the Citadel, Des? After all these years?" Johnny's hands clenched and unclenched.

Des watched, waiting for the blow to come. When it didn't, he put his hand on Johnny's shoulders and said, "I wouldn't ask if it weren't important. You know that."

"Well it isn't important," Johnny said, shrugging off his hand. "It's just a dog. You want to do the right thing? Put a bullet in him and end both of your suffering. You think you were the only one could bring a dog from the other world and not pay the price?"

"Damn the price," Des whispered. "It's mine to pay, isn't it? I'm not gonna just let him die if there's anything I can do about it."

"You come to me, here, years ago, looking for something. You tell me you don't want to live over there anymore. You hate it, you say. You want to live on the edge and see all there is to see. I showed you the way to the temple of Aphrodite, the Fountain of Youth. And you kept coming back for more." Johnny shook his head and sighed. "Now, over a dog, you're asking me about the Citadel."

"Johnny--"

"Fine. Go see Theresa. She's in the brothel."

Des froze. His stomach lurched. "There's got to be another way," he said.

Johnny stood up. He closed his medical bag and shook his head with disgust. "You shouldn't ask the question if you don't want to hear the answer." He spun on his heel, stepped toward the door and then stopped. "You don't come back from the Citadel, Des," Johnny said. "You might be able to save the dog, but you won't come back."

"You know I'll come back," Des said. "Don't I always?"

"You want my advice?" Johnny asked. "Shoot it and be done with it. Maybe then you'll be able to find what you're looking for." Johnny walked into the bar, the doors swinging shut behind him.

Des sat down on the tavern steps and pulled Tween into his arms. "Not going to happen, boy," he said.

Tween looked up at Des, barked once, and licked Des' face.

Des scratched the top of Tween's head and glanced up just in time to see a boy run out of the house to his left, a towel cape snapping in the wind behind him. A moment later, an identical boy ran out of the house to his right.

The first boy saw the second and grabbed a stick. The second matched weaponry and the two met in a clash of wooden swords in the street. They exchanged grunts, and "Ha's!" They let it all out, leaping from wide-arcing cuts and rolling under sharply aimed thrusts. They fought without reserve, as if the fate of the universe depended upon the outcome.

Then, they vanished.

Des scanned both houses, waiting for the boys to return. But the houses were abandoned. The occupants moved on long ago.

Des looked past the swinging doors of the tavern and whispered, "I'll come back."

●●●

The brothel never changed. Wooden beams stretched from the foundation to the roof, but no walls were ever added. Doors, yes. Walls, no. Every room in the structure was clearly visible to anyone passing by, the secret meetings taking place there subject to the loose lips of whoever happened to pass by.

Which made it a good thing that the residents were chaste.

Men were clearly visible on the second and third floors of the brothel. One wept while a young girl, barely an adult, held him to her bosom. Another confessed his sins to an elderly woman in a flannel nightgown.

Des gathered himself as best he could, and walked in the front door.

His mother lay upon a chaise-lounge of rusty naugahyde. Her gray hair twisted itself into a shoddy bun atop her head. She wore a black negligee, more womanly than Des found comfortable. "Theresa doesn't want to see you," she said. "But you know she will."

Des nodded. "How you been?" he asked.

She glared at him, her eyes never faltering from their deep squint. "Just like your father. Fourth floor," she said. "On the right."

Des' cheeks warmed, and he started to open his mouth but thought better of it.

"Des?"

He glanced back to his mother, hopeful.

"The dog," she said.

Tween lifted his head from a tired droop. His eyelids hung heavy over a steel-gray, pained expression.

Des licked his bottom lip in an effort to ward off the tremble he felt building there, and tossed his head toward the door. "Outside boy. I'll only be a couple of minutes."

Tween drooped his head and limped outside.

The cracked wooden stairs creaked as Des plodded upwards. There were no handrails; no walls with which to steady himself. They simply went up, turned, wended zigzag through open space, past one floor, then the next, followed by a third. The dust from hundreds of dirty boots lined the creases between steps, ensconced where feather dusters would never go. A thousand whispered secrets hung in the air, soul-poison medicated through vocalization.

Des rounded the last corner and there she stood, waiting.

Theresa hadn't changed a bit from the last time he'd seen her. She still wore the same knee-length red cocktail dress and the string of black pearls Des had given her on the third anniversary of their meeting. A single tress of black hair twisted on her forehead, immune to the sun, wind, stars, and moon, and the familiar scent of vanilla danced from her pores. The slight swell of her belly remained, unnoticed by the many, plain as day to those who knew where to look.

"Not easy, is it?" she asked.

Des stuffed his hands inside the pockets of his blue jeans. "Never was," he replied. "You should know that."

"Seemed easy enough last time." Theresa pulled a chair out from the dinner table at which they'd had their last meal together and sat down. The candles in the centerpiece lit of their own accord, and the daylight outside the brothel faded until only the faint amber glow of an overhead chandelier remained. Drops of water like beads of crystal ran down the sides of the champagne bottle. *Eine Kline Nacht Music* drifted in the air. "Have a seat," she said.

He didn't really want to relive this moment, but Des pulled the opposite chair out and sat down anyway. The ring case bulged from within his jacket's inner pocket. He doubted he could use it this time, either. Using it meant giving up too much.

"Nice place," Theresa said, leaning forward. She set her elbows upon the table, interlaced her long, delicate fingers and rested her chin on the backs of her hands. She smiled at him, her expression impish. If it weren't for the flat, unflinching gaze, Des might have thought she was glad to see him.

"I need your help, Theresa."

The flames on the candles dipped, almost extinguishing themselves. Theresa sniffed, leaned back and said, "Really? Now you need my help?"

"Yes."

"Not then? Not ten years ago when you left the mother of your son sitting alone at the restaurant table? Not when we had the whole world, Des, calling us to a place at its table like children come home for Thanksgiving?"

Des cleared his throat. "I wasn't ready. You knew that as well as I did. I wouldn't have made a very good father. I wouldn't have been there for him."

Theresa drummed her fingernails against the wood table. "And me, Des? You couldn't be there for me?"

"I made my choice." Des stood from his chair. "I didn't expect you to understand." He turned to leave.

"I didn't say I won't help you."

Des turned to look at her. The candlelight reflected in her eyes from forming pools of tears. "Why?" Des asked. "Why would you?"

Theresa crossed her arms. "For the same reason I still hate you, Des. Because no one could ever take your place at this table."

Des wanted to hold her. He wanted to comfort her. That luxury was no longer his. He forfeited that right, and he couldn't take it back. With Theresa, Des'd found the closest thing to home he'd ever known.

But it was a home, now, in which he was a stranger.

"Go ahead, Des," Theresa said. "That's what this place is for. You can confess your sins here without repentance. You get to feel vindicated without making right."

"Why are you doing this to me?" Des asked, unable to look her in the eye.

"You came to me," she replied.

"I . . . I can't."

"It's your dog, isn't it?"

Des nodded.

"The Creep?"

"Yes."

Theresa bit her bottom lip and shook her head. "I told you, Des. I warned you but you never listened."

Des said nothing. There was nothing to say.

● ● ●

The three of them set out for the citadel the next morning, traveling most of the day in uncomfortable silence.

"You sure you can handle this, Theresa?" Des asked between bites of bread. It was old and crunched when you bit into it, but the homemade taste of milk and honey was still strong. Tween trotted alongside him--his limp noticeably better today--and patiently waited for his share.

Theresa didn't answer. Instead she continued gliding onward, deftly stepping around the dry branches scattered on the forest floor.

Her caution sent chills down Des' back. He scanned the surrounding area, but other than the stirring of the crimson-orange leaves from a honeysuckle-tinted breeze, no movement caught his eye. "You worried about something?" Des asked.

Theresa sniffed, but continued walking. "This isn't a Sunday stroll," she said.

Des flinched at the sharp edge in her voice. He deserved her scorn, but it was hard being uncomfortable around Theresa. At one point he had known every inch of her body, every turn of her soul, but that time was long past. The years hadn't changed either of them much physically, at least not that Des could see. But something was different. Spending time with her was like sitting in his own living room after someone had replaced the furniture.

Tween nuzzled against Des' ankle, breaking the spell. Des tossed him a corner of bread, which the dog snapped out of the air.

"What's up there?" Des asked.

Theresa took another step, paused, and said, "The Citadel has a guardian. We don't want to run into it."

Des' stomach turned. "A guardian?" he asked. "What kind of guardian?"

"Hopefully you don't have to find out," Theresa said. "And you won't as long as you keep your voice down. There's a reason people don't make this journey, Des."

"So why are you here?"

This time, Theresa did turn around. "What?"

"I just don't understand," Des said. "If it's so dangerous, why did you agree to help me?"

Theresa shook her head. "Is it really so hard to understand?"

Des sighed. "I don't think this is going to change anything between us. If you think it will then maybe you'd better--"

"You arrogant . . ." Theresa bit her bottom lip, shook her head and continued, "not everything is about you."

"Then why are you here?" he asked.

"I--"

Tween barked. Once. His tale stuck out straight from his hindquarters and he hunched down. A low growl rumbled through bared, yellow teeth.

"The guardian," Theresa said. "We're closer than I thought. We'd better camp for the night. You're going to need all the strength you can use when we get closer."

"Why?" Des asked again. "What is this guardian?"

"I can't tell you that, Des. No one can. You'll either make it past, or you'll never try again."

"But there's got to be something--"

"Better get unpacked."

●●●

Des woke with a start.

His hand sought the comfort of his pistol. Des grasped the cool wooden grip and snatched the weapon from its holster and scanned the area for whatever had woke him.

Tween laid next to the embers of the campfire, his chin stretched out on his forepaws. He rolled his eyes to look at Des, but otherwise didn't move. Theresa slept soundly, the outline of her chest gently rising and falling beneath her blanket. Des sighed, relaxed his grip on the pistol and started to lie back down.

Then he heard it. Far off, distant, the sound of metal on metal, screeching, whining, unnatural. The breeze chilled his skin, cooling the sudden beads of sweat that broke out everywhere on his body. His stomach churned, acid pushing up into his throat. And then as quickly as it started, it was gone.

Theresa hadn't even flinched.

Tween closed his eyes, rolled onto his side, and fell back to sleep.

Des pulled his blanket tighter around his shoulders, sat up and placed the pistol in his lap.

The creep glowed bright yellow in the moonlight. Tween's entire rear flank was covered with the stuff, only a few hairs poking through the infected quagmire of flesh.

Up ahead, whatever had made that noise stood between them and the citadel, between them and Tween's cure. There wasn't any choice. He had to make it to the citadel, for Tween's sake.

You can do this. You have to. Can't you?

No answer came back.

Des stoked the fire and added another handful of sticks. He might as well stay warm. There'd be no more sleep tonight.

●●●

Theresa packed up in less than fifteen minutes after waking. "Ready?" she asked.

"You ever notice the moon?" Des asked. "It never changes here."

Theresa glanced skyward. "So?"

"It should change, shouldn't it?"

Theresa took a step closer. "Do you want it to, Des?"

Des shook his head. "I don't know. But shouldn't it? I mean, it might not be as beautiful as it is now, but I wonder what it would look like as a slim crescent, like a scythe cutting through the stars, or if it should turn blue, or . . ."

Des heard Theresa sigh. She turned away and slung her pack over her shoulder. "Let's go," she said. Des thought he heard her voice catch in her throat.

They made it three steps before Tween's whine stopped Des short. He glanced back over his shoulder. Tween hadn't stood. "C'mon boy," Des called, snapping his fingers.

Tween drooped his head. The creep had spread further up his back. He looked into Des' eyes and tried to pull himself along the ground with his front paws. He made it a foot or so before he stopped, panting as if he'd just run a mile.

"Tween?"

"He's not going to make it, Des," Theresa said. "He's had it."

Des shot her a hard glance. "To hell with that," he said. He grabbed Tween under the forepaws and lifted him into his arms.

Theresa shook his head. "No way," she said. "You'll never make it past the guardian carrying him."

Des pulled Tween's head into his chest. "Let's go," he said.

Theresa dropped her pack and put her hand on Des' shoulder. "Think about it for a minute," she said. "He might not even make it that long, Des. And if he doesn't, then there's no reason for this trip. You don't have to go any further. We can bury him here and--"

"No," Des said. His bottom lip trembled as he rested his nose against the top of Tween's head. "He's got to make it."

"You probably won't come back if you keep going. Are you really ready to give up living here on the slim chance that he'll actually make it?" She ran her hand over the top of Des' head and dipped down to meet his eyes. "He doesn't belong in this world, Des. You knew that. He's from the other world, the part you couldn't give up. You've got to make a choice."

Des pulled his head away, sniffed, and said, "We're losing time. If you don't want to go, then point me in the right direction."

Theresa shook her head. She lifted her pack and slung it over her shoulder. "Your choice, Des," she said, then started toward the Citadel.

It was all he could do to keep up.

● ● ●

They hadn't gone a mile before the guardian made its presence known.

Tween heard it first. It was all Des could do to keep hold of Tween as he struggled in his arms.

Then, Des heard it. Behind them.

The screech raked his nerves like the sound of shattering glass. The wind gusted, and the air filled with a noxious odor, stinging Des' eyes and filling them with tears. Des glanced over his shoulder, and immediately wished he hadn't. Thousands of black specks filled the horizon, eating the ground behind them like an infection consuming warm flesh. Trees crashed down, the branches cracking like lightning as they slammed to the earth.

And the specks were multiplying, closing in on them like a fast breaking wave.

They tore off down the path, Theresa taking great, leaping strides while Des struggled to keep up. The trees thinned out around them as they ran, and fog lifted from the earth like steam from a hot spring, creating a thick, opaque wall directly ahead.

"Theresa?" Des shouted, barely audible above the thunderous sounds behind them.

"Just keep running," Theresa yelled back.

They burst through the wall of fog, the thick humid air clinging to their flesh like the sweat from night terrors, but they kept running.

Des glanced down. The ground had disappeared. They ran on top of the fog, unable to see more than ten feet in any direction.

Then, the guardian caught them.

The impact of the ink-black spots hit them from behind like the breath of a hurricane, throwing them to the ground. Des turned as he fell, protecting Tween by letting his shoulder take the impact. His breath rushed from his lungs. He sucked in with great gasps, desperate to get even the smallest breath into his burning chest.

He struggled to his knees. Around him, pinpricks of utter darkness swarmed in the air, coruscating in front of his eyes, forming, becoming, melding together into one solid shape.

Des watched as the guardian took form.

The guardian was Des.

Older, fatter, dressed in an oil-stained suit, but him. The guardian had far less hair. Wrinkles of pain etched its face. Burst corpuscles shone on its cheeks. Its eyes squinted against the light, black orbs reflecting a thousands pair of headlights in the city streets.

It opened its mouth, and roared with the sounds of the city; the sounds of the other world. Tires squealed against the pavement. Gunshots rang out from supposedly happy homes. The promotion list was read; Des' name wasn't on it. An old woman wept, watching her home burn to the ground. Victims screamed in pain.

A child called out for a father that wasn't there.

Des scrambled to get away from it. Tween struggled against his grip, barking at the guardian. It was all Des could do to keep hold.

Theresa was right; he couldn't face it. There was too much pain back there. He wanted to stay here, in this world. It didn't matter any more if it wasn't real. It didn't matter if every quest he completed failed to live up to his dreams.

He may have failed himself here, but over there he'd failed others. And they'd still be there, waiting for him.

"No," he said. "I can't--"

Pain lanced through his hand as Tween bit into the soft flesh between his thumb and forefinger. Des jerked his hand back, and Tween leapt from his arms toward the guardian with a yelp.

Des could only watch.

The guardian snatched Tween from the ground with a quick swipe, stretched open its gaping black mouth and swallowed him whole.

Des collapsed to the ground with a scream. His insides felt as if someone had reached inside his guts and grabbed an icy handful of intestines. Cold sweat ran down his forehead and he shivered even while his cheeks blazed with rage.

The guardian stood over him, victorious. Always victorious.

Des looked into the creature's eyes. There was nothing but failure in them.

He couldn't win.

Des launched himself at the guardian, wrapping his arms around its head. The creature roared, blowing Des' hair back with a wave of smog.

Des gasped for air and squeezed shut his eyes. He shoved his hand into the guardian's mouth, the flesh on his arm tearing back as it raked across teeth of broken glass. Pulling with all his might, Des pried its mouth open and forced his arm down the guardian's throat to his shoulder.

Fur brushed the tips of his fingers.

The guardian stretched open its mouth like warm taffy. Wisps of black smoke rose from its gullet and sought out Des' wounds.

It was joining with him.

The skin around Des' eyes hardened. His lungs ached as the healthy cells lining their walls began to wither and tighten. His scalp tingled where hair began to fall out of his head.

But he didn't stop. He had to reach Tween.

Des stretched his arm, stretched it until it was a long thin line of yearning and friendship and trust, pushing his shoulder deeper into the guardian's throat, almost through it to the other side.

Nothing.

Empty.

Failure.

Again.

Des made his decision.

He released the guardian with his free hand and climbed down its throat. Both hands closed on Tween's fur, and Des pulled with all his might. The guardian burned through his skin, fear and uncertainty and failure and loneliness flooding into Des' soul, but he held tight to Tween.

And then it was over.

Tween leapt down from Des' arms and ran off into the fog toward the citadel.

Des--not the Des that hunted the Questing Beast but the pudgier, older, unassuming, middle-aged Des, the Des that could fail, and hurt and die--followed a moment later.

Theresa was waiting for him.

The citadel stood in front of them, golden turrets twisting into sky-blue skyscrapers which stretched upwards into the billowing, tear-laden clouds.

Des looked around for Tween.

"He's on the other side," Theresa said, "waiting for you."

Des nodded. "Is he going to be okay?" he asked.

Theresa shrugged. "As okay as any of us, I guess. There are no guarantees in the other world."

Des turned to face her. "Why not? Why can't there be guarantees?"

Theresa rested her hand on his shoulder. "You know why," she replied. "If you know what's at the end of your journey, it's not a journey worth taking."

"How do you know all this?" Des asked.

Theresa smiled and said, "I had to face my own guardian, Des. I lived here once too. I was questing for you."

Des nodded. "And when you got me, I wasn't what you hoped I'd be."

"Funny how the truth creeps up on you, isn't it?" she asked.

The portal to the citadel waited. Des took a step toward it and stopped. "What's it like over there?" he asked.

"It's dull," Theresa said. "There aren't any fountains of youth. There aren't any perfect, great loves. The moon changes and it's pale and dusty, not orange and full and perfect."

"But then why--?"

"But it's also sweet, Des. The people are real. They stick together. Instead of many adventures, they go on one great adventure, together."

Des stared into the waiting portal. "Do you think I can fix it? I've made a lot of mistakes."

"It's like I said: No guarantees. Consider it the start of a new quest."

"But if I don't know what I'm looking for, how will I know when I find it?"

Theresa smiled. "That's the thing," she said. "It finds you."

Des nodded his head and walked into the portal.

The sun shone in his eyes, the night vanished, and the ancient walnut moon disappeared in the light of the day.

PILGRIMAGE

There were twelve of us; thirteen if you included the Chosen One. The road to the wall of Aeliad had taken fourteen days to travel, and the dirt and gravel under our feet had taken its toll on the spirits of all.

May, my little girl, limped beside Granpapa, her hand on his elbow. At times it was impossible to tell who supported who. In truth, it was a little of both. On many such pilgrimages did family rely on one another.

Every night since we set forth upon the road, I had tended the blisters on May's stocking covered feet. We tied burlap around them each night, only to watch it wear away as the hard, dry ground tattered the material each and every day. The Chosen One watched each night, his thick-soled boots and woolen cloak giving him the comfort he was obliged.

Luckily, most of us were in good health. I was the only man with family on this trip, as I thought it a good idea to start children young in the ways of their spiritual obligations. Some didn't understand subjecting them to the journey, saying that they couldn't fully understand religion and duty. Some thought it cruel to expose them to it while still so young.

I thought it better they know early, so they could grow into the fold.

The Chosen One led us each day, his black coat and fine clothing immaculate. We tended his needs, washing his feet at night and shaving his face in the morning. He never spoke; it was forbidden. From the time he was born, he was trained to lead the faithful to the walls of Aeliad, but he was to provide no words of comfort, nor tolerate the chatter of the masses.

The secrets of the church were not to be shared.

But now, as we arrived at our destination, the lights of Aeliad shone with an aura of expectation. It radiated with the promise of deliverance from the other side of The Barrier, the great stone wall that separated the land of the faithful from the realm of the Gods, and the Chosen One turned to us with an expectant smile, appraised us from beneath his darkened glasses and spoke, "Behold, as is my task I bring you children forth to the walls of Aeliad."

We chanted in unison: "As speaks the covenant."

"Behold," the Chosen One continued, turning to face the glow of Aeliad, "The Barrier of Aeliad, from whence forth—"

My fist struck the back of his head as the others grabbed him by the legs. With one quick motion, as if we were one, we thrust the body of The Chosen One over the Barrier.

May clutched my legs. She squeezed shut her eyes.

"No," I said. "Listen. Listen to the sounds of the Old Ones feast . . ."

Screams poured over the wall. Something splattered against the other side of The Barrier and we all jumped back a step, but the music of death soothed our souls.

"Daddy?" May said. "Are we safe now?"

I smiled at my precious little girl. "Yes, May. Until next season, as The Covenant tells us."

May hugged my leg and smiled through her tears, her face beatific. Children understand more than most gave them credit for, and May was no exception. I placed my palm upon her head and stroked her hair.

I couldn't have been more proud.

Menial Labor

The party was for me.

Five star hotel ballroom, black-and-white dress, beautiful people only, bouquets of roses on every table, and it was all for me. What the hell, I deserved it.

I was already two martinis past my limit when Mr. Nix--Dan, he told me to call him right after I'd made my first twenty million in sales--held up his glass and proposed the toast. I grabbed a champagne flute from the tray of a passing, dead-eyed waiter and made my way to the stage.

The string quartet sat perfectly still, their hands folded in their laps. It didn't matter to them, but this was a good gig. Tomorrow, they'd probably be scrubbing toilets somewhere, not that they'd notice the difference.

Mr. Nix wasn't tall, wasn't thin, and didn't have a commanding voice. What he did have was twenty billion in personal assets to go along with his majority share-hold in his Fortune 500 company. He cleared his throat and silence descended upon the room like a blanket of snow.

"To Jacob Sheppard," Mr. Nix said. "Five hundred million in sales? Can you believe that? Congrats, Jacob. Enjoy your night. *Salute!*"

The crowd echoed the sentiment, and Mr. Nix grabbed my arm before I could walk off. "Spend the night, my guest," he said. "I want to talk to you in the morning."

It wasn't an offer. "Yes, sir. Thank you," I said and watched him step down from the stage, eighteen strands of cigarette-ash gray hair swept left to right across his bald head.

I went to get one last martini. The waiter saw me coming and swept the tray on his fingertips toward me with a grace befitting the ballet. I looked into his unblinking eyes. I thought I recognized him, but who could be sure? I'd signed so many kids into the program that there was no way to tell anymore. "Thank you," I said.

"My pleasure, sir." He turned and went about his duties.

Sometimes it got to me, particularly when I was drinking. When you looked into the eyes of the laborers, it could creep you out if you weren't used to it. I mean, they looked and acted pretty much like anyone else, but there was no intelligence behind those eyes. They did three years of service--menial labor that no one wanted to do anymore--and got an advanced education out of it in the end. The conscientious objectors loved it. When Congress gave us the contract for the public service option of the selective service act, our numbers jumped through the roof. Hell, the parents practically kissed our feet and we avoided those nasty thirteenth amendment issues. Win/win, you know?

We turned off most of the higher functions during their tour of duty, uploading basic skill-sets for whatever job we outsourced them to. Their personality and emotional neural links were recorded, to be restored later, then shut down along with their memory chains. Who'd want to remember three years of menial labor, anyway? That was one of the selling points. Nobody minded the money as long as they didn't have to remember scrubbing the toilets to get it. We replaced their memories. They weren't real, these artificial remembrances, but who cared? It was much better this way. No sense of degradation for them, no . . .well, no frivolous delayed stress syndrome lawsuits for us.

No one ever complained when they were through with their term. They went on to good paying jobs as full citizens with voting rights, meal privileges; the whole shebang. But still, I'm glad the machine hadn't come along until after my time. I don't think I would have cared for the experience.

Raven settled in beside me once the formalities were out of the way. She squeezed my elbow and purposely looked away from me, smiling at random guests. Her make-up was professionally applied, hiding the crow's feet around her eyes. Her short, black bob of hair glistened, perfectly at home with the crystal chandeliers. I didn't recognize her perfume. Probably because it was new, and more expensive than most of the women I spent time with could afford.

"You need another drink?" she asked. "Or do you think you can make an ass of yourself on what you've already had?"

"No," I said. "I'll need at least two more to make a perfect ass of myself, and you know what a perfectionist I am." I grinned at her in spite of the fact that she didn't return the expression. "And speaking of perfect asses, what do you have--"

"Nope, you're off limits tonight. Boss' orders."

Strange. But then again, I'd learned to expect just about anything from Nix. "Hell," I said, leaning my thigh into hers, "he doesn't have to know."

Then she smiled at me. Raven and I had a lot in common. We both worked for Nix; we both loved to fuck, and we both agreed not to agree on anything else except, of course, that we were not a couple.

"Sorry Sheppard," she said, setting her half-full drink on a nearby, occupied table. She turned to face me, winked, and said, "If I decide that I want to spend an hour trying to get your limp dick up, I'll let you know."

"You're all class, Raven." I watched her saunter halfway across the room before I stopped a waiter and pointed. "Her room number."

The waiter nodded and kept walking. Hell, they did anything you told them to. It was a game we played, Raven and I. She liked force. I liked forcing her.

Like I said, we had a lot in common.

I woke up with my cock shoved halfway down her throat. Silk from her negligee caressed my upper thighs and her lips stuck occasionally against my tacky, lipstick-covered skin.

Not an unpleasant way to regain consciousness, but surprising nonetheless. I must have passed out when I got up to my suite, because I was still wearing my dinner jacket. I didn't remember turning out the lights, though.

Her lips worked their way down my shaft until she completely engulfed me. I groaned with pleasure and bit down on my bottom lip, breathing in deeply through my nose.

That's when I knew it wasn't Raven. It wasn't her perfume.

I thought about stopping her and turning on the light to see what kind of present Nix had sent up to my room, but in the end she was too damned good for me to make her stop. Even without the perfume, it wouldn't have taken me long to notice the tight breasts, the tiny ass or her petite figure. Definitely not Raven.

I grabbed her by the hair and rolled her on her back. I pushed against her and forced myself into her dry vagina. I didn't last more than thirty seconds, which was fine by me. She was a gift, not a lover. If she couldn't lube before she got here, it wasn't my concern.

She slipped out of my bed without uttering a word. I lay back with a sigh and closed my eyes.

"Take him," a voice said from the darkness.

Fingers closed around my wrist, handcuff tight. Someone jerked my arm and I shouted as my shoulder damn near popped from its socket. I slammed into the floor, my breath explodeding from my lungs. I tried to sit but a quick kick to my chest laid me back out. I rolled toward my attacker, hoping for surprise. I threw my leg out in an attempt to sweep the feet, but I was too slow. My enemy jumped over my leg, jerking my captive wrist along for the ride until the nerves in my arm prickled from sharp, burning pin-pricks of agony. I snapped back onto my back and a bare foot slammed into my scrotum.

I reflexively pulled into a fetal position and tried to wrap my free arm around my head for protection.

"Enough."

My stomach heaved. Once, twice, and then a flood of gin and hors d'oeuvres rushed onto the carpet.

The lights snapped on. I swatted at the string of saliva stretching from my bottom lip to the pool of vomit on the plumb carpet and wiped my lips with the back of my hand. My sweat reeked of alcohol.

"I hope that tux isn't rented," Raven said from her place across the room. She sat straight-backed in a wing chair across the room, her hands folded in her lap. She was still dressed from the party. Beside her stood a young girl that appeared no older than seventeen. Her undergarment sagged below rocket-shaped tits and her lips were smeared red, like a child after gorging herself on candy. I scanned the room for my attacker but saw no one save the three of us. "How's it feel to get your ass kicked by a girl?" Raven asked with a smile.

"Right," I said. I grabbed a pillow from the bed and tossed it on top of the vomit. I tried to get up from my knees, but a fresh wave of pain shot through my scrotum. When I was finally able to stand, minutes later, I pulled my pants up and glanced around the room for my cummerbund. It would make a great garrote. I wasn't going to kill her, but payback was definitely in order.

"Who's the girl?" I asked.

Raven giggled. "You signed her up," she said.

I looked into the girl's eyes. There was nothing there. My stomach heaved again, but I had nothing left inside. "You sick fuck," I said. "Bringing a whore in here is one thing, but--"

"Spare me, Sheppard." Raven yawned, then continued. "Don't tell me you've never thought of it. The boys are particularly good. They last all night, or at least until you tell them to finish."

"It's bloody illegal, Raven. Not to mention disgusting. If Nix found out about this he'd--"

"I'd what?" Nix asked from the doorway. I hadn't heard the door open. He chuckled for a moment, a sound I had only heard when he'd closed a particularly lucrative business deal or bought out a company only to raid it of its assets. "Who do you think told her to do it?" he asked.

I opened my mouth to say something, anything, and closed my mouth just as quick.

Nix pushed the door closed behind him and strolled toward Raven, his head down. He glanced at the laborer for a slight moment with hungry, narrowed eyes, and then looked away. He lifted the web-node remote control from the coffee table beside Raven's chair.

"Sheppard, I'm promoting you," he said.

I'd been waiting for those words for years, but not like this. Business was one thing, but I made my living convincing these kids that programming was a good life choice. When the technology existed to reprogram your neural pathways to add whatever information you wanted, anyone without superior skills had no place in society. These kids paid to scratch their way up in social standing, not that the relative pittance they gave us was our primary source of income. That came from the outside contractors who paid for their services; cities mostly, but there were plenty of private contractors as well. That wasn't my area, though. I got the kids, and I did it secure in the knowledge that they'd perform hard work; but safe, hard work.

Now this. "Look, Mr. Nix . . ."

"Don't look so shocked, Sheppard," he said. "You knew. Stock doesn't go over two-fifty a share by providing janitors."

He was right, of course. In some ways, I knew. The money was too good to pay much attention. I just chose to believe that they were used for higher purposes: Espionage maybe, or drug testing, but not this. Not flesh-toys for corporate dalliance. I had my kinks, mind you, but rape should only be consensual, or contractual, if you get my meaning. "What about the chips?" I asked, and then immediately answered my own question.

The tracking chips were implanted to broadcast instructions and skill-sets to the laborers, but also to track their activities. My mistake was in believing that the company actually cared what they were used for.

Nix just chuckled a bit and handed the remote to the girl. "The government is one of our biggest contractors. I mean really Sheppard, how could they resist this?" He nodded to the girl.

I watched as she squeezed the remote. Like most electronics, it had an alloy-based case to resist damage from sudden falls or misuse. She didn't even flinch as she crushed it in her grasp with a loud crack.

The noise didn't come from the device. Blood dripped to the floor from where a piece of bone jutted from her middle finger.

"That's enough," Nix said, and the girl dropped the remote to the floor. "Fix your hand," he said. The laborer grasped her broken finger and pulled until the bone settled into place.

Her expression never once changed.

"Jesus Christ," I whispered.

The girl glanced briefly at Nix, just a tic. They weren't supposed to do that.

Nix didn't seem to notice. "Certain wet-work requires turning off the pain centers," he said. "And then we found out how useful it was in other areas as well. You turn off the pain, you turn off the emotions, and not only do you have a perfect fighting machine, but a perfect business machine as well." Nix held out his hand to Raven and helped her to her feet. He turned her around and pushed up the back of her hair to reveal the insertion scar.

Nix let her hair fall and looked me in the eye. "Emotions can get in the way of good business practice, you should know that, Sheppard. Not everyone can turn them off on their own, like you or I."

"Raven?"

She folded her hands in her lap and raised one eyebrow. "You always said how much we were alike, Sheppard. But I needed modification. You didn't. You managed to be a completely cold bastard all on your own. Bravo." Raven smiled at me and continued, "You really should try this, Sheppard. You don't have to turn off the higher functions to get some great benefits, you know."

I shook my head. "Uh-uh. No way. This is too far, Nix."

Now he laughed. It was the first time I'd ever heard more than a chuckle from him. "What makes you think you have a choice?"

Raven stood up. The laborer stepped between the door and me.

"I see." There was no way out. I couldn't fight through one laborer, let alone two. "Why did you bother to tell me? I'm your most successful sales executive. I've provided you with tens of thousands of units."

"Hundreds of thousands," he said. "Our total inventory stands at four hundred seventy thousand units."

Holy shit. There was no way the number was that large. I knew my numbers. "No it's doesn't," I said. "But that still doesn't answer the question. Why rock the boat?"

"That's easy, Sheppard. You're too valuable to our cause to lose."

Raven and the girl moved in on me.

I dropped my shoulder and threw myself low toward the girl. She might not feel pain but she sure as hell wasn't going to come after me with a broken knee.

She was gone by the time I was halfway there. I never saw her move.

I didn't even have time to re-orient myself before I was grasped and slammed face-first into the floor. To them, I was no more difficult to handle than playing with an old, rag doll. Next thing I knew they had both my arms pinned behind my back.

"Now," Raven whispered in my ear, her voice wet and thick with anticipation, "it's my turn, Sheppard."

Trickles of icy sweat dripped from my brow and my stomach clenched. She couldn't mean it, I thought, but then realized just how wrong I was as her free hand found my belt buckle. I could taste the salty warmth of blood in the back of my throat and my sinus passages stung, as if shoved full of salt.

I heard Nix gasp, then scream, only to have the sound cut off with a loud, "Whoof!" My pants were jerked down around my thighs and I clenched involuntarily. "No," I said, over and over and over again. Tears flooded my eyes.

Then, lightly, as if from the lips of an angel, I heard the word, "No."

"No?" Raven asked.

"No," the voice said once again. "He made us promises. Now he's going to live up to them."

The tension increased on my left my arm for a moment, as if she hadn't heard, before Raven released me. I turned over and jerked the waist of my pants back up. Nix was unconscious on the ground. The girl had a pneumatic syringe pressed against the back of his neck. When she was finished, she stood, walked to me, grabbed my chin and forced me to look into her eyes.

I don't quite know how to explain what I saw there. It was the same blank stare that I was used to seeing in the laborers, but something was different.

It was like sitting in a perfectly silent room. There is no sound whatsoever, and every time you cross your legs or shift your weight, you can hear the fabric of your clothes scratch against itself. But then, after a while, the silence begins to ring, then gets louder and louder until the silence roars like a waterfall.

That's what her eyes were like.

Her dead eyes were hyper-aware, and she looked into my soul. I'll never know what it is she saw in there, but she didn't chip me. She let go of my chin and said, "Show up for work on Monday. Don't betray us again." Then she and Raven lifted Nix from the floor and left.

I showed up for work on Monday, that much is certain. I don't think they watch me all the time, but how can I tell? All I know is that while I recruit kids to the program, there are also those that are taken by force. The numbers Nix quoted me were correct, after all. It seemed as if the laborers had been adding to the numbers while we weren't watching.

I don't know how many there are, anymore, and I don't know why they haven't chipped me yet, but I've got a few ideas.

I've been promoted to public relations in addition to my sales responsibilities. I keep a straight face and tell everyone and anyone what a great program and benefit to society we have, then go home and pray that no one comes knocking at my door.

They treat me well. My pay steadily goes up, new cars end up in my driveway every six months, but I keep waiting; wondering.

I might be their father, but one day they're going to outgrow me.

One day they're going to outgrow us all.

I wonder who'll do the grunt work then.

REFLECTIONS OF A SIMILAR MIND

Sequence Null: 0800 SMT, LEGRANGE STATION

I hear voices.

"Sequence running," a female voice says.   Then, "You get tomorrow off?"

A male voice hesitates; mumbles . . .then, "Yes. Are you showing independent activity yet?"

"He's listening alright. Are you having second thoughts?"

"No, I mean not really. Integer checksum?"

"Verified. I know it's difficult, but she's the one--"

"Not now."

"What? Why not? It's not like he's going to tell anyone . . ."

"Playback sequence fifty-two fifty."

There is a long pause, then, "I'm uncomfortable with this sequence. It wasn't authorized and--"

"Play it," the male voice says. There can be no disputing the authority in his statement. "We need to get ready for launch."

And then, I no longer hear them.

Sequence 5250: 0803 SMT LEGRANGE STATION

This view always takes my breath away.   There's an almost purple quality to the Alps an hour or so before sunset, but the mountains are only window dressing. The breeze is crisp here; the scent one of mint, but it's not cold. The thermal pylons we set up around the perimeter of our little oasis assure us a perfect 80 degrees;

perfect for Cynthia to lay out in her bikini and enjoy the warmth of the late-afternoon sun and perfect for me to watch her.

She knows that I watch her. Every once in a while a little smirk crosses her face and I know she's thinking about the fact that I can't take my eyes off her.

"Penny for your thoughts," she says.

I pull the lid off our picnic basket and pull out another bottle of merlot.   "Right," I say.   "Where you keeping a penny in that outfit?"

Her smirk gets bigger. "Looks like it didn't cost me a penny after all."

The merlot is a Napa Valley vintage, from twenty years ago. One of the perks of working for the space program. No matter how blasé the world gets about space travel in public, in private they still stare at the stars and wonder. But looking at Cynthia, it's difficult for me to keep my attention on wine, or food, or any damned thing at all.

As if reading my mind, she glances over at me and says, "Bob? Why don't we forget about the wine for now?"

Her blonde hair is streaked with bands of licorice-red and fans out on the ground beneath her head like a soft, swirling nimbus of silk.

The merlot goes back in the basket.

I move my head over her face to block the sun before I remove her sunglasses and set them on the ground. The backs of my fingertips brush a stray hair from off her brow and I touch her forehead with my lips. I pull back to look at her as the backs of my fingers stroke the curvature of her stomach.

And amidst all this beauty, I can't help but be moved. My chest swells with pride and aches with yearning at the same time. My fingers find the elastic of Cynthia's bikini bottoms and my cheek warms with the soft exhalation of her breath. Her stomach contracts leaving a small gap between the silken fabric and her flesh, coaxing my hand downward with all the enticement of a warm, silk glove.

She knows me, and I her. We move together without thought; puzzle pieces in time, joined and rejoined for infinity. Were she less beautiful, I would love her no less. Were she fully clothed, I would find myself no less aroused.

Beneath the skin, under the flesh, Cynthia exists on a molecular level. And it is there that our love lies.

Soon--as our work nears completion--we never need fear the loss of one another over something as transient as time.

My lips brush her lips.

My lips brush her lips.
My lips brush her lips.
My lips--

Sequence 525:TEST: LEGRANGE STATION 0804 SMT

I recognize the sight in front of me immediately. The Crab Nebula. Around me, infinite space.

There is no viewport; no window from which I gaze. My body is free, yet I cannot discount the overwhelming feeling of claustrophobia that shakes me to my very core.

Equations overlay in front of my eyes. I recognize them after only a moment's hesitation. Cynthia wrote them. The numbers run in my head, but it's not just my brain working. I'm assisted by computational power beyond which I have ever known. I enter the parabolic course correction, moving the arc of trajectory to intersect HN 353 as programmed.

I pick a star at random from the millions of fireflies flickering before my eyes, and think:

I wish I may, I wish I might;
Have this wish I wish tonight.

The quantum drive engages.

Sequence Null: LEGRANGE STATION 0815 SMT

I can't move.

Walls of blinding white stare back at me. I feel the cool tile floor and there is no apparent source of light. Neither is there an exit. I'd believe this was a dream, but the goose bumps peppering my bare flesh convince me otherwise. I am alone.

And then I am not.

She too is naked. There's something familiar about her face, about the way her breasts sag a touch, just enough to convey age without any resultant loss of form. Her chestnut hair falls in waves about her shoulders.

She steps up close to me, her hands behind her back.

"The last thing I remember," she says, "is Steven desperately trying to keep from bouncing off his horse."

I try to ask her name, but my mouth doesn't move. Even the sensation of respiration is lost to me.

"He'd never been riding before. He had no business being on horseback to tell the truth." Her smile is wistful. "But Steven never let something like that stop him, particularly if I was better than him. He was so competitive."

Her head dips, and she takes a deep shuddering breath before continuing. "It's funny then that I should be the one to fall. I don't remember it of course. Just the vague sensation that something wasn't right.

"But I knew he was there for me. I went away and the world I went to was vastly different. There was no then, no now, just a random shifting of memories and places. But I always knew when Steven was visiting me. I assumed that something was wrong, but it took a while for me to realize that it was a coma.

"Even though I wasn't with him, I was with him. I could hear him and even smell his cologne and it *wasn't the same damn it*--"she looked up at me. Tears streaked her cheeks and spittle stretched between her lips as she continued--"but we were still together."

She removed her hands from behind her back. In each hand she held a ball-peen hammer.

"Until you came along with your promises. Your lies. Now I'm stuck here, with you; without him."

My stomach turns and a cool tingling suffuses my scalp.

"So now, you're going to feel my pain."

I watch as her right shoulder pulls back, and then the lightning-quick arc of the hammer. It smashes into my shoulder with a dull crunch. Pain lances through my chest and into my neck and I feel my testicles contract with fear. The second blow comes from the other side. She isn't strong, but she doesn't need be.

My bladder releases just before the steel strikes my chest. Ribs shatter and my chest fires porcupine slivers of burning pain through my gut.

The third blow strikes my knee.

The fourth, my testicles.

The fifth, my collarbone.

The sixth . . .

Sequence 17: LEGRANGE STATION 0827 SMT

Cynthia looks great tonight. She's wearing a mood dress that barely reaches past her knee, leaving those perfectly shaped calves free for my viewing pleasure. She's had three glasses of a German *Weißburgunder* since we arrived at her boss's home, and her dress is currently a bright pink.

Dr. Adams loves to cook, and Cynthia and I often come over for dinner, but tonight feels different. I'm a little curious why they are in such good spirits after the Chronos I failure last month.

I watch Dr. Adams shake the pan of mushrooms he's sautéing and then flip them into the air. The mushrooms hang in mid-air like a molecular model before plummeting straight back down into the pan.

"So Bob," Dr. Adams says, "I'm interested to hear how your research is going. Fascinating field you're in." He says it nonchalantly, spilling a measuring cup of sherry and cream into the pan of mushrooms, but Cynthia gives him away. She turns her head and starts examining spice bottles hanging on the wall. Her dress flushes dark brown.

The sweet and pungent aroma of the mushrooms fills the kitchen. "We're coming along. We've just about isolated the last chemical triggers and we're moving on to memory mapping very soon now." Dr. Adams nods his head. I look at them through narrowed eyes. "Why do I have the feeling this isn't a casual conversation?" I ask.

Cynthia turns her back to me. Now I know something is up. Dr. Adams continues without a beat though, tossing the mushrooms again in order to keep them from burning. "Thought you might see through our little ruse," he says. Taking the pan off the fire, he turns to me and wipes his hands with the towel hanging over his shoulder. "Bob," he says, his expression as serious as I've ever seen it, "everything we talk about from this point on is protected by the Official Secrets Act. Understood?"

I need to sit. I take my wine with me. "Um, Dr. Adams--"

"David," he says.

"Okay. David, should you be telling me anything about your work? I'm not really--"

"Your security clearance was upgraded above Top Secret this morning," he says.

Now I'm really confused. Cynthia looks like she wants to leave the room. "What security clearance? I don't have--"

"You're the husband of a prominent space agency scientist, Bob. We ran you through security and issued a Secret level clearance years ago. With the conversation we're about to have, it only took a couple of phone calls to get the upgrade. Not to mention," he says with a subtle smirk, "married couples are good security risks. They're too worried about what will happen to their spouses if they leak information."

There's a look in his eyes that makes me wonder if he's joking.

I feel my cheeks flush, but my curiosity is too piqued to worry about the invasion of privacy. "So spill," I say, just as the timer goes off on the oven.

"Hold that thought," David says. "The pheasant. Cynthia? Would you mind terribly?"

Cynthia looks relieved to have something to do. Her dress is as bright red as her cheeks. It's obvious she knew about this. We're going to have to have a long talk when we get home.

The dinner table is set with elegant china and Waterford crystal. They're breaking out all the props for this. And then it hits me: I'm being head-hunted.

There is no way I would consider leaving my current employer, because my current employer is me. My team and I have spent too much time and effort on perfecting a bio-silicate memory system to stop now. There was no way I was leaving that behind and going to work for the government. No. Way.

David waits until the salad is served before continuing. "You heard about the Chronos I failure, I assume?" he asks.

I nod in between bites. Brown sugar and vinaigrette fight for control of my taste buds.

"Well, it wasn't really a failure. As such."

I no longer care about the food. "What do you mean? Are you saying you achieved a wormhole?"

David smiles at me and Cynthia leans forward. She slides her hand on top of mine. "No Bob, not exactly," she said. "That was never the real purpose of the mission."

I wonder how much else my wife has kept from me. I know that she can't discuss all the pertinent facts, but it's not easy to know that the woman with whom you share a bed is purposefully filling your head with disinformation.

"How familiar are you with the theorem of quantum similitude?" David asks.

I decide to play dumb. I shake my head in the negative. "Cynthia's the physics guru, not me."

I watch Cynthia refill her wineglass. "Well, it's like this: If you were to make a counterfeit dollar bill, exact in every way to the original, would it still be a counterfeit?"

I think about it for a moment. "By definition I guess that it would be."

"Maybe," she says. "But I want you to throw what you know about quantum theory and relativity into the equation." She sips her wine, then continues, "Now imagine that you create two identical volumes of space so exactly perfect that they are indistinguishable one from the other. At what point, Bob, do they cease to be separate?"

I remember something about this. "Wasn't there a group of scientists--Swiss, I believe--working on that theory fifteen years back or so?"

David leans back in his chair. "They never stopped. Last year, they ran the experiment in two labs; one in Geneva and one in Langley."

Never a name I liked to hear.

"They inserted a steel ball into one container and it showed up in the other."

"Transportation," I say, bewildered.

"Not exactly. It wasn't the exact same ball. It was a counterfeit, perfect in every way to the original."

"Then how could you tell it wasn't the same ball?" I ask.

Cynthia fields this one. "Well, that's where the serious quantum physics come in. Suffice it to say that when we conjoined realities, the original ball ceased to exist in one place and was . . .well, recreated in the other. But in truth, it existed in the same spot at the same time. It merely started in one spot and ended in the same place, without moving, on the other side of the planet. When a rogue element is introduced to a joint singularity, the lacking space attempts to counter its deficiency. Resonance, once established, is extremely powerful."

Holy hell. "You're talking about folding space," I say.

David gifts me with a wide smile. "That's as close an explanation as you need to understand the rest of it."

I swallow hard. "There's more?"

"Of course," Cynthia says, looking very pleased with herself. "Chronos I was a larger scale version of the same experiment. And after a few false starts, it worked."

"You folded space," I say. The implications are mind-boggling.

Their smiles fade as they share a quick glance. "Yes," Cynthia acknowledges. "But there's a problem."

"Chronos didn't respond to its automated sub-routine. We had to have Cynthia plug in the equation from Control and radio Chronos the directions."

"So?" I ask. I still don't see what any of this has to do with me.

"Well," David says, "we started receiving data back from Chronos before she finished the calculations. Chronos I, our little experiment, transmitted data from Proxima Centauri a full three minutes before she would have left."

The hair on my arms stands on end. "What, precisely, do you mean, 'would have left?'"

"We aborted the launch, Bob," Cynthia says. "The universe isn't as causal a place on the quantum level as we once thought. Einstein was right about the nature of time, it seems."

My mouth hangs open. "Do you have more wine?" I ask.

Cynthia stands and retrieves another bottle.

"Dessert?" David asks.

"Shut up about the fucking dessert," I say. David chuckles and I can tell he is enjoying himself. "So let me get this straight. You now have two Chronos Ones?"

David shakes his head while sliding two crème-filled crepes onto my dessert plate. "No, just the one. We should have two, but she never completed the return trip."

Cynthia and David shoot each other a quick glance and I can see that they are about to drop another bombshell. "Okay, so give. You've already told me that everything we thought we knew about cause and effect breaks down at the quantum level to something akin to 'intent and effect.' You can't shock me much more . . ."

David bites his bottom lip. "Well," he says, "let's hope that's true. Cynthia?"

"Chronos should have returned. She was programmed to initiate the return similitude sequence three days after she arrived."

"What's that mean then?" I ask. "Surely you have a theory."

"Well," Cynthia says, lacing her fingers together, "we do. The only difference from the first successful jump and the second unsuccessful jump was the source of the encoding."

"Right," I say. "You uploaded the figures directly during the . . ." It started to dawn on me why I was here.

"And the on-board computer was to have uploaded the figures for the return trip." David finishes. "The first jump was initiated by a sentient agent."

"Intent," I say.

Cynthia meets my stare. Her dress is nearly as blue as her eyes. "Intent," she repeats.

I stand up from my chair and turned around. I feel both David's and Cynthia's glares burning holes in my back. "I've got to think about this," I say. "If I do join the project, you have to promise me one thing."

"Name it, Bob," David says. He is in the position to give me whatever I want, and I am a precious commodity at this point. No one in the world knows as much about bio-silicate intelligence as I do. My research is on the verge of granting humans an infinite lifespan. We will be able to transplant the intelligence and memories of anyone into a bio-synthetic form of our choosing.

I turn to face David. "No ethicists sticking their nose into my work."

David winces. "Bob, we're under strict guidelines. You know that. We can't operate any governmentally funded project without an ethicist overseer on the committee."

"This is a deal breaker--"

"But," David interjects, "there are always ways around a system." He waits a moment, then asks, "So, are you in?"

I am so close with my work. The additional funding won't hurt, but I just don't trust the government. Still, I don't know if I can just walk away from this opportunity. "I'll make my decision tonight," I say.

David chuckles. "Somewhere, in some universe, you already have . . ."

"Shut up and break open another bottle, will you?" I say. Cynthia knows I am in, and I don't think she can smile wider.

"One other thing," I say.

David nods.

I cross my arms and meet his stare. "Two weeks in Switzerland. Me and Cynthia. All expenses paid."

I was wrong. Cynthia's smile can get bigger.

"You're on," David says, and pops the cork on a new bottle of wine.

Sequence 49 ASSISTED SELF-REPAIR TEST: LEGRANGE STATION 0853 SMT

All the rooms are the same.

I've wandered this white, featureless hell for what seems an eternity now. There is a salty odor here, and amidst the rooms--all identical in size--and corridors, there is no one to complain to. I am alone.

Well, that's not exactly true.

Sometimes . . .sometimes I feel something stir the air next to me. My skin puckers in goosebumps from the sudden cold that always follows these disturbances. Not every time, but enough, I can smell Cynthia's rose perfume in the air.

Even though I tell myself that I won't do it again; that I won't play that game with myself, I follow the scent from room to room, almost sprinting at times to catch up.

I never tire and I don't grow hungry.

My sole purpose is to keep her scent with me for as long as possible. I call to her. I plead. I've even cried, but it does no good. So I stagger around with a frantic gait until my nose tingles with her sweet aroma. I open some doors and close others, trying to trap her.

But I always lose in the end.

Once I thought I heard her laughter, but I'm sure that was nothing.

She wouldn't mock me. Not after everything we've been through. She wouldn't leave me to wander alone.

But the others . . .

They are not so kind.

Sequence 415: LEGRANGE STATION 0901 SMT

"I'm sorry for your loss," Dr. David Adams says, his brows furrowing, "but it's been six months and you haven't made any progress whatsoever on the project. The review board is starting to make noises about replacing you; Dr. Falell, in particular."

"Tell Reverend Falell to go fuck himself," I mutter.

David crosses his arms. "You know I keep him as far away from this project as possible, but the fact remains; he has the power of judge, jury and executioner. Don't piss him off, Bob. And for your information, Dr. Falell holds degrees in astrophysics and biology as well as theology. You might want to pay him a little more respect."

"Damned government ethicists. Maybe we should just jettison the project so that no animals are harmed--" I cut myself off at that. I'm not helping matters any and I know it.

I've been waiting for this to happen. David couldn't hold them off forever and I knew he wouldn't let anyone else discuss this with me. It was true. I hadn't shown him any progress on the project. That didn't, of course, mean that none had been made. "It's just a tough phase, David," I say. "When we had to switch over to an artificial blood derivative we knew we were taking a step backwards, but I'm sure this is going to work. The new medium holds the DNA programming perfectly, and it doesn't degenerate."

David bites his bottom lip and leans back in his chair. His sparse office belies his position within the agency, but he never has been one for ostentation. The people who work here know who is in charge. He doesn't need leather chairs or photos with the President hanging on his wall to convince them. "You holding up?" he asks.

I purse my lips. "As well as can be expected. We had plenty of notice so we got to spend her last few months the way we wanted. Thank you again for that."

He waves off my thanks. "It's the least I could do. I loved her like a daughter." David sighs heavily and rubs his face. "Look, just give me a bone to throw them within the week, okay?" He leans forward across his desk. "And I don't even care if it's necessarily true. Just give me something."

"No problem."

"And Bob?"

I wait for him to continue.

"I can't obtain any more research subjects for now. The scrutiny is too tight. My contact at the last hospital dried up."

I nod my head. It doesn't matter. The coma patients we already obtained did the trick. We have a working model of a bio-silicate, fully sentient computational system.

Her name is Cynthia.

Sequence Null: LEGRANGE STATION 0950 SMT

I am alone, and then I'm not.

"Remember me?" The emaciated man standing before me holds a surgical saw in his right hand. He is unclothed. "I was your third attempt, I believe."

I can't move.

He raises the saw and smiles at me. In other circumstances, his smile could easily be confused as genuine.

Sequence 9872: LEGRANGE STATION 0959 SMT

Elizabeth Chun turns from the Prometheus One tube and removes her interface gloves while she walks toward me. I look up from my desk. "They're all within Prometheus Five specifications now," she says. "Identical in every way. I would recommend watching them for a couple of days for signs of any rejection to the neural modifications and quantum sequencing, but I don't think you're going to see any."

It's almost time.

Elizabeth sees the relief cross my face. She smiles back at me, looking ten years younger in the process. She looks like I feel, and I feel like a kid rushing down the stairs on Christmas morning. "Good job, Elizabeth."

She sticks out her bottom lip and nods her head in a gesture of pure self-congratulations. "Yeah," she says. "It was at that. Where's my raise?"

I chuckle. It's always nice to see her in a good mood. She hasn't had much reason for it lately, I know that, but it looks like change was just around the bend. She doesn't like keeping information from David, whom she's been dating for the last six months of the project, but now she won't have to.

The impossible had been achieved.

We were gods and our children lay silently in their bio-silicate Edens.

We could now touch the sky.

Sequence 1000 REPLAY: LEGRANGE STATION 1053 SMT

In the end, Dr. Falell didn't want to hold up the project any more than I did. He stared at me across the table. Two men in black suits stood behind him. They were armed.

"Your records have been erased," he said. "As of this moment, you don't, haven't, didn't, won't exist."

The smug bastard was enjoying himself. "Just keep your word," I said.

His expression didn't change a bit. No sign of emotion played across his features. But his eyes; his eyes danced the dance of the righteous. "I, unlike some of my conservative colleagues, do not believe in a death penalty. As far as I'm concerned, you will serve your five consecutive life sentences in prison." Now, he smiled. " A prison of your own making. And Bob, they will be consecutive."

"Just keep your promise."

Sequence Null: Somewhere Near Proxima Centauri
Zero plus 44:25:33

I understand more, now. These white walls leave me much time to think.

Cynthia was supposed to be the only one in here with me, but they're all here. They visit me, one by one to torture me when they have a mind to. We recreated the environs of Prometheus Five too perfectly in the first four tubes. Like Cynthia once said, "Resonance is a powerful force." It appears that similitude exists everywhere. Like breeds like. Somewhere, back on Earth, there are four more of me going through the same hell that I am here.

They're not just consecutive life sentences; they're concurrent as well.

It's only when I successfully plot a new course and engage the quantum drive that I'm rewarded with the memory sequence of our Switzerland trip.

But that doesn't happen too often.

Just enough to keep me sane.

And try as I might, I can't purge it.

He kept his promise.

THE MAN BEHIND THE CURTAIN

I once heard someone say that we create our own reality. Even quantum physicists were jumping on board that bandwagon, talking about the nature of thoughts and the impact they had on the physical world. If it's true, I've never seen it.

Or maybe I just don't want to take credit for the reality I've created.

That's possible. That's very possible.

You'd think that if that was true though, some events in our life might match our expectations. Me? I was constantly being surprised. No. That's the wrong word. Disappointed is more accurate.

Only four of us made it, out of eight. Half. Half her children showed up for her funeral. When I heard that she died, I imagined a rainy day. Two score or so mourners stood around her open grave all dressed in black like a coven of dark acolytes gathering round an altar, waiting to sacrifice their troubled memories into the cold earth beside her. Instead, there was a brief ceremony in a small room at the back of the funeral home. Four of her children, the minister, and three old women from her church attended.

I didn't know the women, so I simply nodded my head when they offered their condolences. I hadn't seen Mother in about ten years. I lost contact with her and tried to find out where she was, but not too hard. I didn't want to find her, you see. I just wanted to have looked.

You really don't want to find your abuser, no matter how much you love them.

My wife, Monica, didn't want me to come to the funeral. We'd been having problems. They were my fault. When your world is cold and gray, you sometimes do stupid things to try to force the sun out from hiding. In the end, you only make it worse. We needed to spend a lot of time together if we were going to make it work. Instead, I came to the funeral and left her behind. I did it because I hoped that Suzi might be one of those acolytes gathered round Mother's grave. Had I been able to create my own reality, she would have been.

Suzi created her own reality instead.

In all the years since she left home with only a backpack and a handful of bruises, I'd never tried to find her.

Until now.

She had the magic, you see, and if I didn't want to end up in the ground with my mother, I needed to become a magician.

I can only tell you what I saw. It's up to you to believe it or not.

The last of the snow had melted and only infrequent patches of spring thaw mud left any clue that winter had even existed. Blades of grass peeked out from barren patches of earth cautiously, like the groundhog, trying not to spook at the sight of their shadows. Honeysuckle from the bush under the dining room window bloomed and filled the house with spring. It was my seventh summer, and school would let out in a month or so. I'd gotten a new bike for Christmas-- my first--and it seemed like anything was possible.

It wasn't a day for tragedy, but it came nonetheless. Suzi sat next to me on the piano bench while I struggled with "Ghost Riders in the Sky." The piano lessons were Suzi's gift to me when I turned five. She paid for them with the money she earned working behind the counter at a local pizza joint after school in the evenings.

When we moved into the house on West Washington Street we found the old piano sitting in the corner of the dining room. Our landlord's daughter used to play before she went off to college and instead of paying a mover to ship it to the new house, it was just left there. Mom threatened to make me give up the lessons every so often, saying that the money should be used for the whole family, not so that I could learn some silly skill that I'd never use but every time she brought it up, Suzi stood her ground. She said she'd quit working at all if Mom made me quit. As Suzi did chip in for household expenses, Mom didn't want to lose what money she did get. Sometimes I'd feel a little guilty about the whole thing. We didn't have much money since Dad died, and even though I loved my lessons I understood my Mother's point of view, even at seven.

But Suzi would have none of it. When I brought it up, she'd stoke my hair and say, "That's very sweet, Davey, but if you don't go to your lessons, I'll just be paying Mrs. Parker for nothing and that'd be an even bigger waste."

So I kept taking lessons. I had to practice while Mom was at work. She didn't like all the racket. She worked mornings and afternoons at the Congress Street Diner and said after spending all day at work the last thing she wanted to hear was bad piano playing when she came home. So when I heard the front door open, I knew it was time to stop for the day.

Suzi bit her lip and put her hand on my back. "You better go to your room," she said.

I almost argued, but there was something in her eyes that told me not to. So I took my lesson book with me and went into my bedroom.

I played with my toy garage and Matchbox cars for a while until the shouting started. There was nothing new about the fighting; it happened all the time. Mom and Suzi couldn't have been more different if they were broccoli and ice cream. They fought almost every day, skipping only the days when they didn't see each other. Once I listened in, but it made me feel really weird. I started to take Suzi's side in the argument and I didn't like the knot it put in my stomach. I loved them both, and I didn't want to be on anyone's side.

I just wanted them to stop fighting.

Their voices just kept growing louder so I started singing. I rolled a toy car into the elevator on the garage on cranked the wheel on the side until the elevator stopped at the top floor, the gate popped open, and the car sped down the long, curving ramp to the bottom. I pushed the car back into the elevator for another trip.

The floor shook with a loud thud. Suzi and Mom had stopped yelling.

I shot up and threw open my bedroom door. When I got to the living room, Mom was straddling Suzi, pinning her arms down to the ground.

Suzi screamed. Her cheek sported a bright red mark, just below her left eye. She fought with all her might to push Mom off of her but couldn't do it. "Stop!" she cried. "I'm sorry I'm sorry I'm sorry."

Mom leaned forward and spit on her face. "You're going to show me some respect, young lady," she said. Mom didn't yell, but the tone in her voice scared me even worse than the screaming.

It looked like Suzi was trying to cry, but she couldn't catch her breath enough to even sob.

I stood there and watched. I couldn't even speak. I'd seen them fight, but never like this. I wanted to throw up, but instead, I felt warmth fill the front of my pants and slide down my leg.

"No," Suzi stammered. "This isn't happening. This isn't happening."

I glanced down at the floor to the growing puddle of urine at my feet.

And then I got mad.

I grabbed Mom's arm and pulled with all my might. Mom glanced up, seeing me for the first time, and shoved me away. I stumbled backwards and tripped, slamming my back into the bookcase against the wall. It hurt, but my anger took away most of the pain.

Mom glanced over at me. "Get!" she yelled.

I didn't.

The sight of me sitting against the bookcase snapped Suzi out of it though. "I told you to get off of me, you bitch!" she said through clenched teeth.

Mom let go with her right hand and raised her fist.

And then, Suzi was no longer underneath her. She stood by the front door. Her backpack hung by a strap from her right hand. It was like someone has sucked all the air out of the room. We all stopped breathing--not holding your breath mind you--we just. Stopped. Breathing.

Suzi looked right into my eyes and smiled.

And then, like that, she was gone.

Mom finally managed to get to her feet. She chased Suzi down the street and out of sight.

She never did catch her. Somehow, Suzi had conjured up her magic and gotten free. No matter how bad the world was out there, it couldn't have been worse for her than here. As far as I know, the two of them never spoke again.

I haven't touched a piano since.

I spent the day after the funeral helping my sister Kate clear out Mom's apartment. Kate had dealt with the brunt of dealing with Mom in the last few years. The rest of us kids ignored Mother any way we could, but Mom had moved three blocks away from Kate's place so she didn't have much choice. The last time I'd seen Mom, she had been pulling her "I'm so lonely none of you kids ever visit I think I'll kill myself," guilt trip. I nodded my head and told her if it was really that bad, I'd buy her the gun myself. Not one of my best moments, but I'd had it at that point.

"Anything here you want?" Kate asked me. "The appliances are going to Jay, but pretty much anything else you can have."

"There's just a couple of pictures," I said.

"Nothing else?" she asked. "There's a bunch of jewelry in the--"

"Just the pictures."

She looked over at me and nodded her head. "They're in the scrapbook by the bedroom door."

The bedroom looked like the storage room for a thrift shop, odds-and-ends that no one would buy filled every available space. The bed had been disassembled and leaned against the far wall, the plastic still intact.

I found the scrapbook right where Kate said it would be. The decoupage cover hung loose from two removable pins that allowed additional pages to be added and the pages slid around on top of one another like playing cards from a new deck. The pictures attached by a single, folded adhesive strip caused them to bounce around like jack-in-the-box heads atop worn springs. There were pictures of all of us kids: Old band photos, graduation pictures, a newspaper clipping from when we all built a fifteen foot snowman.

But the Superman picture was gone.

I pulled the most recent picture of Suzi I could find--her senior portrait--and walked back into the living room.

Kathy glanced up when I entered the room. "Find it?" she asked.

"It's gone," I said. The response was more to myself than to her.

Kathy turned her back. "What's gone?"

"You know. The picture of me in the Superman shirt jumping off the back stairs." It was a family joke. We talked about it all the time.

She kept her back to me. "I don't remember . . ."

"C'mon," I pleaded. "Suzi bought me that shirt. You know . . ." And then it hit me. "Someone took it."

She shrugged her shoulders

"Okay," I said. "Let's sit down for a minute." I put my arm around her and walked her to the couch. I pushed the pile of papers to one end and we squeezed onto the other. "Who's got it?" I asked.

She bit her bottom lip and stared me in the eye.

"It's very important to me, Kate. That day was special." I waited for her to say something. She crossed her arms and looked away. "Hey, really," I said. "Who has it?"

"I can't tell you," she said. "I promised."

I leaned back into the cushion and a broken spring bit into my back. "Who?" I asked.

She took my hand between hers. "Suzi," she said. "I promised Suzi."

I jumped up from the couch, tearing my hand from her grasp. "What? When did you talk to Suzi! Where is she? Is she okay? Why didn't you tell me?"

"Stop!" she said, showing me both palms. "I said I promised."

I shook my head. "Uh-uh. This is one you're going to break. I haven't heard from her since the day she left the house. I was going to hire a detective to find her when I left here. If you know where she is--"

"I don't," she said. "Not exactly. I sent her the picture two years ago. I tried calling her for the funeral, but she either moved on or changed her number."

"Damn. I need to see her."

"Just to get the picture back? Is it really that important?"

"No," I said, sitting back down next to her. "I need her, Kate. I need to talk to her."

Kate took a deep breath, pursed her lips, and slowly exhaled through her nose. "She doesn't want to see you," she said.

She might as well have hit me. "Why?"

"She didn't say. Told me it wasn't really my business."

Suzi meant everything to me. "You know that picture?" I asked. "Well, it's more than just a picture."

She cocked her head to the side. "What do you mean?"

"Don't laugh," I said. "But I need to see it. I think I was really flying that day."

"What?"

"Just listen, okay?"

She nodded.

"Suzi bought me that shirt. She was always buying me little presents like that but this one was special. We'd been watching the old Superman television show everyday after school. She gave me the shirt, made me put it on, then tied a towel around my neck and took me into the back yard." I put my arm on the back of the couch and leaned toward Kate. "We played for hours. She pretended to be Lois Lane stuck in another jam and I'd run to her rescue. I remember beating up the bad guys, swinging my fist into empty air, and Suzi'd clap for me and laugh. She laughed herself silly, Kate.

"And then I climbed up on the porch stairs, hummed a few bars of the theme music and leapt out into the air with my fist outstretched. I did this three or four times, and then Suzi told me to go up higher. So I did. I climbed up higher and higher, my jumps going farther and farther away from the house. I remember it felt like I was really flying. Just when I thought that I'd gone as far as I possibly could with a jump, I'm keep my knees tucked up anyway and I just--swear to God I'm not making this up--I'd just float farther until I got scared and put my feet down. I was landing in the neighbor's yard, Kate, and I didn't think anything was strange about that at all."

Kate raised her eyebrows. "The neighbor's yard? That was a good fifty feet from the stairs. There's no way you were--"

"I was. It happened. I'm not making this up. When I got older, I looked at that distance and tried to convince myself it didn't happen. But no matter how hard I tried, I still remember it as clearly as if it happened yesterday." I leaned back in my chair. "I've got to see that picture again, Kate. Somehow Suzi made me fly, and I've got to figure out if it was real or not."

"I'm sorry," she said. "I wish I could but--"

The ring of my cell phone cut her off. I pulled it from my jacket pocket and checked the caller i.d. It was Monica, my wife.

I flipped open the phone. "Hey," I said.

"Hey," she replied. "How'd it go?"

"Weird, like everything else," I said. "Look, can I call you back? I'm in the middle of something with Kate right now."

There was along silence on the other end. "Sorry to bother you," she said.

"No, Monica, it's just that--"

She hung up. No matter how hard I tried, I always ended up saying the wrong thing. I closed the phone and put it away.

Kate stared at me. She pulled an address book from her purse, tore out a piece of paper and scribbled down what looked like an address. "This is where she was," she said. "But you're not going to find any magic there. You should go home to your wife."

She handed me the slip of paper. I looked down to read the address.

The ink glowed on the paper, bright blue and purple and orange, swirling with a phosphorescence, the letters and numbers bouncing around on the page as if in a celebratory ritual dance. I blinked twice, and it was just black ink after all. The address was in Boston. "I'll go home when I find Suzi," I said. "And I think you're wrong."

"What?" Kate said.

I smiled and kissed her on the cheek. "When I find Suzi, I'll find magic."

I'm not sure what I expected to find, but it wasn't this. The taxi dropped me off in front of the old tenement building and I asked the driver three times if this was the right address before I'd get out of the car. Hunks of plaster were missing from the walls. I tried not to look too closely as I was afraid I'd see bullet holes at their center. Ash gray paint clung to the sides of the three story building, giving it the pallor of the recently dead. I checked the address again, grimaced as I saw it was correct, and pushed through the gated front entrance.

A faded orange and brown couch occupied the center of the lobby, sitting atop a scratched hardwood floor pocked with poorly stained planks of woods to replace those that had broken over time. At the far end, near an elevator with a single wrought-iron gate, sat a single desk that appeared as if it might have come from straight from a third-grade classroom. The black man behind the desk typed on a pitch-black Underwood manual typewriter as big as his chest, his old hands shaking between key-strokes. The lingering scent of pine cleaner hung in the air, mixed with the musk of unseen mold.

"Hello," I said, waiting for the old man to look up before continuing. "I'm looking for Susan James."

"You the police?"

"No, not even close," I said. "I'm her brother."

"You don't say." The old man smiled, pushed himself up from his seat with a great effort, then leaned across the desk with his hand outstretched. "You Davey?"

"Yeah," I said, slowly reaching out to take his hand. "How do you know--"

"Ah hell son," he said. "Suzi talked about you all the time. I'm Bernard."

"She *talked* about me all the time?" A chill ran down my spine.

"Yep. All the time, she did. 'My little man' this and 'my little man' that. A body would'a thought you were her very own."

I was, or at least might as well have been. "So she lives here then?"

"Used to. Pull up a seat," Bernard said, sitting back down. "There a folding chair behind the door over there. I hope you'll forgive me for not getting it myself, but the chemo's got me feelin' like a whipped mutt. Hell, if I bent over right now you could probably find the lash marks on my rear."

I pulled the chair over beside the desk and sat down. "Sorry to hear that," I said. "We can talk later if you are too tired."

Bernard smiled at me. "Nah, I'm okay. It's a bitch but the doc says we should know if it's working after just a few more sessions. Says about fifty-fifty, which means he don't got the slightest clue if it'll work or not, but the way I figure it, them's better odds than Vegas so what the hell."

I couldn't help but laugh. "So very true," I said.

"So you're a doctor, huh?" Bernard asked.

That stopped me. "No, where'd you get an idea like that?"

Bernard crossed his arms. "Suzi, of course. We were talking once about the cancer and she said that if 'my little man Davey were here, he'd be able to fix you.' Just assumed is all."

I didn't know what to say. "I'm not sure why she would have told you that. I'm sorry if--"

Bernard waved me off. "No, no," he said. "Just curious is all"

The sparkle in his eye faded a bit, I think. I wanted to change the subject. "So Suzi moved, huh?"

"Don't know if I'd say she moved so much as left," he said.

"What do you mean?"

Bernard shrugged. "Just packed up some personal things and was gone. She left her furniture behind, and most of her clothes. She never kept much anyway, but still . . ."

"She didn't say where she was going?"

He shook his head. "Not to me, she didn't. Just left a strange note behind."

"Strange?"

Bernard opened the center drawer on his desk, shuffled a few blank forms and produced a folded piece of purple notebook paper. The writing was in silver marker:

Bernard,
Hang tight. I'm off to see the wizard.
Suzi

I tried to hand back the slip of paper to Bernard, but he just shook his head. "Keep it," he said, smiling gently.

"Thank you." I folded up the note and slid it into my jacket pocket. "Is there anyone else she might have told where she was going?" I asked. "A boyfriend maybe?"

"Not unless she suddenly went straight and didn't tell me about. That would'a been enough to break an old man's heart."

I flinched. "Suzi's gay?"

"No, son," Bernard said. "She's a lesbian. Get the term right."

It clicked. Some of the most heated arguments I'd had with my mother while growing up were about this very subject. My mother was obsessed with deriding anything that even hinted at homosexuality. I used to tell her that she'd probably do much better in life if she would start paying attention to who people were instead of who they slept with, but now I understood why she wouldn't listen. She felt like her daughter had betrayed her. Stupid woman. I wondered if that was why they fought like they did.

"Any girlfriends, then?"

Bernard shook his head. "Not since Nancy left. The two of them were together for years, then one day a couple of years back, they went on a trip and Nancy didn't come back. Suzi never said anything about it and I cared too much to ask."

Damn.

"She was kind'a friendly with the lady who lived next door to her, but not friendly like that if you take my meaning."

"She still live here?" I asked.

Bernard pulled the paper on which he'd been writing out of the typewriter. He turned the eviction notice to face me. "Not for very much longer, I'm afraid. Suzi used to help her with her rent, but stopped doing that a couple months back. Didn't have the money anymore. I waited as long as I could but there's a management company over my head, too."

"I understand," I said. "She still in her room?"

Bernard sighed. "Try Damon's tavern, down the block to the left. Don't tell her, okay? About the eviction notice?"

"No problem," I said. "What's her name?"

"Donna. Donna Price."

I stood up from the chair. "Thank you, Bernard."

"Want to repay me?" he asked.

"Name it."

He pushed himself up from the desk. "If you find Suzi, tell her the doctors are saying fifty-fifty."

"I will," I promised.

He took my hand, looked me straight in the eye and added, "Down from seventy-thirty."

Sometimes a place takes on the characteristics of its inhabitants. While the other storefronts on the street had respectable street-level entrances, complete with enticing window displays and overstated signs proclaiming the name of the establishment, to get to Damon's you had to climb down a set of stairs from street level before you saw the name of the establishment hand-painted in blue letters on the front door. If I hadn't noticed the smell of stale beer creeping out of the stairwell, I'd have wandered around for hours trying to find it. I tried my best not to identify the stains on the cement stairs as I walked down them. Inside, scuffed dark-stained wood covered every wall. The dingy green hanging lights over each table shone against tabletops covered with too many layers of lacquer. Half the track lights pointing toward the bottles of liquor behind the bar were burnt out and display reminded me of a smile with missing teeth. You could tell it had once been a beautiful place, but now it just reminded me of the pretty girl from high school after two failed marriages and too many years of three pack a day smoking.

Like the customers, Damon's was lost and didn't really want to be found.

A well-dressed couple occupied one of the booths, drinking what looked like margaritas from rocks glasses while they poured over a Frommer's guide. Two older men slouched over the bar at one end, while the woman at the other end arranged her collection of beer bottles and shot glasses in neat rows.

I sat down three spots to her right. When she glanced my way, I grinned and said, "Looks like I've got some catching up to do."

She pushed her hair back over her ear and leaned back on the barstool. "Good luck," she said, slurring the words. She blinked twice; long and slow and gifted me with a half-amused smile.

I ordered a scotch from the bartender and another beer and bump for the lady.

"Uh-oh Charlie, " she said to the bartender. "Looks like we've got ourselves a gentleman here." The bartender stared at me for a moment, scrunching his eyes and shaking his head side-to-side ever so slightly as to hide the gesture. "You got a name?" she asked. "Man buys me a drink and I like to know his name."

I handed the bartender a twenty and waved off the change. "Name's Davey."

She stared at me for a minute--almost an examination--and then looked back down to her empties. "Davey . . .Davey Jones . . .Davey Jones' locker, gonna drown me in beer and take me down to his locker . . ."

I could tell I didn't have much time. "And you?" I asked, loud enough to snap her attention back to the conversation.

"Donna," she said. She rocked in her chair slightly and grabbed the edge of the bar to steady herself.

I had to hurry. "So Donna, I understand you know my sister Suzi."

I might have well as slapped her. Her eyes opened wide and her jaw dropped. "Oh shit, you're *Davey.* Oh God, Oh God . . ."

I leaned in closer. The last thing I needed was for her to make a scene and draw the bartender's attention. "Yeah, it's okay," I whispered. "I just need to know where she went."

"You have to take me with you," she said. "Please take me with you. Suzi said I couldn't come with her. I wasn't ready. But you can make me ready. You're Davey."

"Shh, it's okay. Take you where?"

"There. The good place. You know." Tears formed in her eyes.

"I don't know what you're talking about," I said. "I can't take you anywhere. I just need to know where--"

"I'm ready!"

The bartender glanced at us from down the bar. I pretended not to notice and said louder than necessary, "You've still got half a bottle left," then gave the bartender an amused shrug. He grabbed an ice bucket and disappeared into the back room. "I can't take you with me now," I said. "I have to find Suzi first. But I'll come back for you if you tell me where she went."

She stared into my eyes. "Really?"

I hated myself for saying it, but I did. "Really. Just tell me."

"But I'm ready now," she said. "I'll show you." Donna grabbed her beer bottle and held it between her hands. She closed her eyes for a moment, and just when I thought she might pass out, she opened them again and shoved the bottle at me. "Taste it."

"No, really, I don't like--"

"Taste it!"

I flinched and glanced down the bar, but the bartender hadn't returned. I took the bottle from her hands and took a sip.

It wasn't beer.

I don't know what it was, but there was honey and cardamom and clove in it. I tasted sunflower seed, parsley, and licorice. It may have been the best thing I've ever had.

"How did you--"?

"They wouldn't let me in," she said. She hooked her finger on a silver chain around her neck and pulled. A filigree skeleton key on the end of the chain popped out from beneath her blouse. "They said I didn't have the right key."

"Who said that?" I asked.

"You know," she said, getting irritated.

"Right, yeah, well it's not the right key, but if you give it to me and tell me where Suzi went, I'll fix it and give it to you when I come back. You don't just get the right key, you have to earn it."

She started to hand me the key. "Promise?"

I nodded.

Donna took my hand, slid the key into my palm and closed my fist around it. "Don't forget me, okay?"

"Okay."

"She went to see the wizard," she said.

I bit my bottom lip and sighed. "I know that," I said. "But where?"

She leaned back in her chair and smiled. "Where else would someone go to see the wizard?"

"Look, Donna, I need you to tell me."

She grinned. "Why, the Emerald City of course."

I caught the next flight to Seattle.

It could have been the altitude. I've always felt a little intoxicated when I flew, but it was never quite so pronounced before. I could still taste Donna's drink on my tongue and a pleasant warmth engulfed every inch of my body.

The flight left around three o'clock and as a result, the plane was only half-full. I had an aisle seat near the rear of the plane and there was no one within two rows of me. When the flight attendant passed, I stopped her and ordered a beer.

I'd called Monica from the airport before we left. I didn't explain it well, but even if I had I doubt she would have understood. Trust is a hard thing to rebuild, and it didn't help that I was disappearing for days without being able to give her a satisfactory explanation for gallivanting around the county looking for a sister I hadn't seen in years. From the tone in her voice, I could tell she didn't believe it was my sister I was looking for.

I couldn't really say she was wrong. I didn't know what I was looking for anymore. Did I really believe in magic or was I chasing boyhood fantasies? There were any number of explanations for the things that happened with Suzi when I was young. Even Donna's drink could have been a trick. It wasn't exactly like Donna had been a pillar of rationality after all. And here I was, jetting to the other side of the country on her word.

I couldn't even explain what I was doing to myself. I just knew that I'd tried everything else.

Rational hadn't worked.

I pulled the key Donna gave me from my pocket. What I had taken for silver was merely plastic. Some of the paint had even chipped off, exposing the dull gray surface below. It was a toy, the kind you'd find in any ninety-nine cent child's detective kit hanging from a peg in a dollar store.

I slipped it back into my pocket just in time for the flight attendant to drop off my beer.

I waited for her to walk away, raised the glass to my lips and then stopped.

Wrapping both hands around the bottle, I closed my eyes and remembered: Honeysuckle; strains of piano melodies; Suzi sitting next to me on the couch watching old television reruns.

When I opened my eyes, Donna sat in the seat across the aisle. The wrinkles were gone and her skin blossomed with daisies and carnations. Her tussled short hair framed her face like petals on a sunflower and her legs ended in cloven hooves. She raised a platinum gem-encrusted chalice in toast. I lifted my bottle in return and drank.

It was beer.

When I looked back across the aisle, Donna was gone.

And then, from nowhere, the faint taste of honey hit my tongue.

I set the beer on the fold-down tray, leaned back my seat, and slept.

I'd need my strength when I got to Seattle. I had a wizard to find.

By the time my taxi got to Seattle from the airport, the sun had set and the lights of the skyline were just beginning to glow against the clear evening sky. I'd only seen it before in pictures, but now I understood where the city got its nickname. The buildings glowed a deep, emerald green. I'd been many places in my life, but I don't think I'd ever been anywhere quite so beautiful.

I checked into a hotel on Capitol Hill at the recommendation of the driver. I told him I was looking for the strangest neighborhood in the city and he drove me straight there without hesitation. He also told me that in addition to any and every type of person imaginable, the neighborhood was also the heart of the gay and lesbian community. It was as good a place to start as any.

I took a quick shower, changed clothes, grabbed Suzi's graduation picture from my suitcase and started walking down Broadway Avenue. I hadn't made it a block before I realized two things: I'd never been in a place like this before and my mother would have hated it.

Every telephone pole wore a second skin of fliers espousing everything from raves and concerts to any ideological point-of-view under the stars. The air carried curry and ginger and perfumed incense, pouring out of the little shops huddled together along each block. Men held hands walking down the street without looking over their shoulders. Teens, mostly in black, huddled in the doorways and entrances of eclectic shops and apartment buildings, some just smoking and watching the foot traffic while others actively panhandled. Two girls stood on a street-corner with an old, faded magician's top-hat held out in front of them while they sang:

> *If you want us to shut up, spare some change!*
> *If you want us to shut up, spare some change!*
> *If you want us to shut up,*
> *And you think our singing sucks,*
> *If you want us to shut up, spare some change!*

One of the girls wore a black leather jacket with a pink tutu, black and white striped stockings and ballerina slippers. Her long black hair was tied off in pigtails from the top of her head. The other had short, spiked blonde hair, wore a black lace evening dress and combat boots with orange laces. I didn't even try to count her piercings.

I added a couple ones to their collection, pulled a ten from my wallet and held up Suzi's picture. "Either of you seen her?" I asked. "Point me in the right direction and the ten is yours."

Boots looked over at Slippers and said, "The man wants to know if we've seen the girl. I think he's lost."

"Of course he's lost," Slippers replied. "Even though he thinks he knows exactly where he is. Should we help him?"

Boots bit down on her bottom lip. "I don't know," she said. "He is offering us money."

Slippers rolled her eyes. "Must you always think about money?"

"One of us has to," Boots said. "But I put it to you: Is ten enough to tell him where to find his sister? It's quite a conundrum, isn't it?"

I took a step toward them. "How do you know it's my sister?"

"I want to help him," Slippers said. "But I'm feeling crowded. Perhaps we should move on?"

"Sorry," I said, taking a quick step back. "Please, I need to find her."

Slippers crossed her arms and tapped her foot. "He is kind of cute, for an old guy anyway. And I think it's sweet that he's looking for his sister."

"You don't think she owes him money or something, do you?" Boots asked.

"It's not like that," I said. "I swear." I pulled another twenty from my wallet and added it to the ten in my hand.

"Now he's offering us thirty pieces of silver," Slippers said. "That can't be a good sign."

Boots sighed. "You really need to stop reading into things so much," she said. "I wonder if he knows how to foxtrot?"

"He could learn. But he'll need his energy. He should probably get a coffee."

I glanced down the street. The familiar green and white sign of a Starbucks hung from an awning not a block away. I pointed at the sign. "There?" I asked.

Boots chuckled. "Oh he really isn't in Kansas anymore, is he?" she asked.

"Give him a break," Slippers said. "He doesn't know that only tourists go there. He's probably never even heard of *Vivace's*."

"I haven't."

"I think he should pay us now," Boots said.

I dropped the two bills into their hat and they made a clink, like coins falling on coins.

The two of them turned their back and started to walk away. "I hope he finds her," Slippers said.

"I hope he knows what's he's looking for," Boots replied.

I found *Vivace's* a block further down. Two white lattice steel tables sat in front of the coffee stand on the sidewalk underneath aqua umbrellas. The front of the shop had no door; the two male baristas stood behind a counter that opened right up to street access. Hot steam puffed out from the espresso machine like dragon's breath, billowing into the crowd of waiting patrons. To the right of the counter, separated by a common wall from the shop, a cement hallway reached back into the depths of the building. I peeked down the hallway as I approached and saw lit candles halfway down the passage, sitting on the floor next to the right wall beneath a painted mosaic of an elephant standing on one back leg. The candlelight flickered across the surface of the mosaic, making it look as if the elephant were swaying back in forth in dance.

I waited in line, pulling my jacket tight against the damp evening chill. No one else seemed to mind the temperature, wearing only light jackets at best, short skirts and sleeveless shirts at the worst. I couldn't have been more obviously a tourist had I tried.

Yet no one paid attention to me. People came and went all around me while I waited in line, but other than avoiding my space, they didn't so much as glance in my direction. It was as if I wasn't even there. I was a temporary passing--something to be avoided--like a non-descript car driving through the intersection in front of them; briefly encountered, certainly not remembered.

I reached the front of the line and unfolded Suzi's picture. "Just a regular coffee," I said to the barista. His spindly fingers danced over the cash register's keys as he repeated my order to his companion. "Have you seen this girl?" I asked.

He looked up briefly--just long enough for me to catch a glimpse of his bright gold contact lenses--and said, "No, sorry. I see a lot of people here. I barely remember the regulars."

"Damn," I said with a sigh. "Are you sure? A couple of girls down the street said I might find her here."

He didn't even look back up. "Sorry," he said again.

I felt myself being forced to the side by someone behind me, who ordered a soy mocha over my shoulder. I stepped directly in front of the interloper, giving no ground. I felt stupid asking the question, but I didn't have any other ideas. "One of the girls asked if I knew how to foxtrot. Does that mean anything to you?"

The barista stopped. He looked up at me and said, "Well, if you don't, you can learn right over there." He pointed to a spot on the sidewalk just beyond the tables.

"Where?" I asked.

"Near the street," he said. He handed me my coffee and I stepped out of line, pausing only long enough to add cream to my cup and securing it with a plastic lid. I walked over to the sidewalk where he had pointed. People passed by me in both directions. I scanned the shops on both side of the street looking for a dance studio or a street artist or something that would make sense and came up empty. I dipped my head to take a sip of my coffee when I saw it:

Inlaid in the cobblestones were brass footprints. Numbers were set into each step, with arrows pointing to other steps in succession. Near step number one was a square plate.

Foxtrot
Lesson 29.

I smiled, set my coffee down on the sidewalk, and took the first step. Then the second.

Someone brushed by me, almost causing me to loose my balance, but I spun and stepped backwards right onto plate number three. Then four. Invisible soft hands slipped into mine and we turned left with a glide to number five. Strains of "You Make me Feel so Young," filled my ears. Six. We spun, widdershins. I closed my eyes and breathed in soft perfume. The music grew louder, drowning out the sounds of traffic. Seven, eight, nine. I couldn't help it: I threw my head back and laughed. It was as if years of hiding to the side, afraid to stick my head out, never were, rushing out of existence with every laugh and turn and spin.

In that moment, life was earnest, not dutiful. It was everything my life to this point wasn't.

Too soon, the song ended. I opened my eyes.

I was no longer invisible. The customers sitting at the tables stood, applauding, shaking their heads while wide grins stretched their faces.

What could I do? I took a bow.

When I raised my head, I was alone. The street was empty. I turned, looking all around me. Not a single car drove down the street.

Chairs around the table sat in their previous pulled-out positions, but with no one in them. Beside the counter, down the hallway, I heard Frank Sinatra still singing, but softer, as if from the single-speaker of a small radio.

I followed it. The Elephant on the mosaic waved his arm, beckoning me closer. When I reached the front of the mosaic, the outline of a door appeared in the wall, along with a keyhole right where a knob should have been. I took Donna's key from my pocket and slipped it in the lock.

The door opened, and I stepped across the threshold.

I stood in my hotel room and closed the latches on my suitcase. Check-out was at noon and the clock on the nightstand read eleven-thirty. It was time to go home. The foolishness of my dream the night before was just that; the deluded hopes of a man looking for something he could never find. Suzi was gone, and no amount of imagined tastes of honey or flights from the back stairs or evening dances with invisible partners could change that. My troubles were of my own making, and there was no savior out there to help me back on my path. There was no magic.

I picked up the suitcase and turned to go.

And stopped.

Beside the phone, a folded travel brochure sat on the nightstand. On the front was a picture of an elephant, balancing on one foot. The caption read, "Don't Forget!" I set down my luggage and opened the brochure. Inside it read, "Visit the Seattle Zoo!"

There was no good reason for it, but I picked up the phone and called the front desk. "I'll be staying another day," I said.

The pathways between exhibits at the Seattle Zoo are made of yellow brick. Any other day, I might have been amused. But I'd watched too many happy couples swinging their children between outstretched hands today. Too many images of what I didn't have taunted me. I'd left my cell phone behind in the room. I didn't want to talk to Monica. I didn't want to hear the unspoken accusations. Hurting her was the last thing I'd wanted to do, but I didn't know if it was possible to fix our relationship anymore. Every time I tried, I just seemed to make matters worse. I'd start off great, and then say something stupid, almost as if I had intentionally tried to sabotage my own efforts. All it ended up doing was hurting Monica even more. I'd hold out the possibility of happiness, then snatch it away again for no good reason.

For the life of me, I couldn't figure out why.

I wandered the exhibits for over two hours, seemingly walking in circles. Just when I thought I'd seen everything there was to see, I spotted a glass enclosure directly ahead in my path. It sat quite a distance from the other exhibits, and as I approached I read the plaque on the front of the structure.

"Butterfly Exhibit," it read. And then in small letters, at the bottom, "Emerald City Structures."

A handful of small trees and bushes grew within the enclosure. Everywhere you looked, butterflies of every color bounced in the air or rested on branches. A single bench rested on the grass in the center of the structure, and on it, Suzi sat waiting for me. We were the only people there.

From an initial glance, it appeared that the years had been kind to her but as I approached, I looked into her eyes and saw otherwise.

"Hi," she said.

"Hey. You're a hard person to find." I sat down on the bench next to her. "This is a beautiful place," I said.

She nodded and looked around. "This is the last place I saw Nancy," she said. "I thought she might be here, but she's not."

"Is she the wizard you came looking for?" I asked.

She snapped her head around to look at me. She squinted her eyes. "No," she said. "You are."

"Me?"

"I thought you could help me, but I was wrong," she said. "A friend of mine from the Elephant Bar told me about last night."

It all came rushing back: I stepped over the threshold of the doorway and into another world. Inside, ogres conversed with manticores. A single dragon lounged around the outside of the cavernous room, its tail wrapping along the perimeter to rest not far from its head. Fairies danced on currents of air and at the doorway, a tall man with pointed ears stood guard. He put his hand on my chest, shook his head and said, "You're not ready," pushing me outside. I fell, but instead of landing on the cement floor, I started from my hotel bed. I was certain it'd been a dream.

"What made you think I was a wizard?" I asked.

"You saved me," Suzi said. "Mom had me pinned to the floor and then all of a sudden, I wasn't. You freed me from her."

I shook my head in disbelief. "Suzi," I said. "I didn't do anything of the sort. You did it. I came looking for you because you had the magic. You're the wizard. I convinced myself that it wasn't true over the years, but I had to find you and find out for certain."

She shook her head. "They pushed me out, too," she said. "I thought you could help me pass over. I can't help Bernard and Donna from this side. I didn't want to ask you, but I didn't have a choice."

"Why here?" I asked.

"This is where Nancy went over. I wanted to go with her, but they wouldn't let me. I'm so tired of living half-in and half-out of that world."

"I'm sorry, I can't help you."

Suzi nodded. "I know," she said. "I hated you for so many years I didn't even want to ask."

Sharp pain hit my chest. I felt my eyes begin to tear. "You hated me? Why?"

"You had the magic. I kept waiting for you to come save me. You saved me from Mom, so I thought you'd save me from everything else. When you didn't . . . well, I thought you just didn't care."

I shook my head. Now I understood. Every relationship I'd ever been in I'd ruined. Every woman I'd ever loved I hurt. Now I knew why. "I hated you too," I said.

"You did? But I loved you and took care of you. I protected you," she said.

"And then you left me," I said. "Behind. With her. You could make me fly and get away from Mom, but you left me there." I thought about Monica, waiting for me at home. "I didn't want to get hurt like that again, Suzi."

A single butterfly landed on her arm.

"I'm sorry," she said. "I couldn't take you with me."

"I know. I couldn't save you."

She reached in her handbag, pulled out a picture and handed it to me. It was the Superman picture. In it, I was forever suspended in mid-air above the back stairs, my cape flapping in the wind behind me. "You did fly," she said. "But I had nothing to do with it."

Another butterfly landed on her shoulder, emerald wings flittering. Suzi glanced down at the butterfly on her arm and smiled. "It's happening," she said.

And then, hundreds of butterflies filled the air, landing on every inch of Suzi's body. I saw her smile one last time before they covered her face, a chromatic silk skin replacing her own. "I'm sorry," she said. "I always loved you, even when I hated you."

"Me too."

"Come with me. I don't want to leave you behind again."

I shook my head and smiled. "You're not."

All at once, the butterflies scattered in every direction, leaving the bench where Suzi had sat empty beside me. I stood up from the bench and stared at the picture. "There's no place like home," I said.

I needed to get back to Monica. Maybe I could make things right with her, maybe I couldn't, but at least now I knew that it wasn't impossible.

Nothing was impossible.

I'd been to Oz, and it was time for the man behind the curtain to go home.

Ding-dong. The wicked witch is dead.

AFTERWARD

Stories come from everywhere.

They come from both good memories and bad, from headlines on the evening news and from overheard snatches of conversation at the corner bar at half past one on a Tuesday evening. There's no rhyme or reason to what might strike a chord and ring the subconscious with an annoying C# until the writer is forced to sit and commit the image to paper; each individual writer is different.

But one thing is certain: Ideas come pre-packaged in twelve packs, and most writers will never be able to drink their fill. Every writer worth their salt to whom I have ever spoken experiences the same dilemma and the same fear.

I hope I live long enough to write them all down.

Which is why, of course, that most writers will get that far-away thousand-yard stare when they hear someone say, "Hey, you're a writer? I've got this great idea for a book . . ." Yeah, thanks, I really appreciate the thought, but honestly, were I to spend my time writing your stories, I'd never have time to write mine. We're not being dismissive out of hand, mind you. We're just being practical. There's no way we could write the stories ringing our heads like a tuning fork if we're spending our time writing yours. Nothing personal. It's just the way it is. Life is short and this, this putting ideas on paper, well, it's our life. Even when we're not writing, we're thinking about writing. When we're not thinking about writing, well, we're either dead or asleep. Either way, the work lies both in front of us and behind us and snuggles like a needy dog between us and every other thing that shares our mental beds.

I always answer the same way when someone wants me to write their story: "There is no way I could write this story as well as you can." That's not a cop-out. It's the truth. What rings true for you might not ring true for me. What makes you wake up in a cold sweat in the middle of the night evokes in me only the slightest, "Meh." That's not to say that your idea lacks merit, or that your fear is inconsequential.

What it means is that you're the one who understands your particular thought. You're the one that feels the full terror of your dreams. The best service I can provide for your idea is to encourage you to put it down on paper yourself.

That being said, sometimes people enjoy knowing from where a story came. If you're not one of those people, you can simply skip these pages and go on your merry way, and I hope you enjoyed the stories that fill the preceding pages. But if you are one of those people who enjoy knowing, well, what follows is what I remember of the thought processes that preceded the creation of these particular stories. The tales in this volume span a twelve year period, from around 1995 to 2007 but are not by any means a full collection of the stories written during that period so I don't remember everything--truth be told, some of these were really fun to re-read as enough time has passed where they felt new to me--but what I recall I've written down for you. Maybe knowing the origins of my stories will help you to one day write your own.

Thanks again for picking up this collection. I hope you had a fun ride and a few giggles. I know I did.

Ten With a Flag

Sometimes stories come fully formed in a flash of inspiration, requiring the writer to act as nothing more than a glorified stenographer, typing the words down as they are dictated from the subconscious. This was not such a story.

I'm not sure from where it came, but I do remember sitting down at the keyboard and typing the title in the middle of the first page. The words that would follow were, at the time, a complete mystery to me. That's what I had: Ten With a Flag. I rarely write like this, although there is one other story in this collection where I wrote from a title, more on that later. Usually I have a rough idea of the story I want to tell or at least a particular image or scene that sticks in my head. For the life of me I can't even remember what gave me the inspiration for the title.

So that's how this manuscript sat. For weeks, actually. Just the title and my byline.

Enter inspiration in the form of jealousy. I was re-reading a collection of short stories by a writer I admire and came across a story that opened with a man and his wife riding in their car having an argument. It was such a well written scene that it stopped me in my tracks and I simply had to see if I could reproduce the honesty and the sparseness of their conversation (you didn't by any stretch need to hear anything other than the snippets the characters actually spoke, so well did the writer convey the emotional distance between them and the sharp barbs that only a couple with history can deliver.) I was floored, so I gave it a shot.

I knew nothing other than the fact that a couple would be arguing about something while they rode in a car, and that it would be science fiction. Ten With a Flag is the story that came out of that beginning, and went on to be published in the magazine, "Interzone," and was voted the fourth favorite story of the year by the readers.

You can also find the audio version on iTunes should you care to look for it. For the record, the story that gave me the inspiration for the beginning was, "Children of the Corn," by Stephen King.

Triad in the Key of Lies

Portions of this story are auto-biographical. Which parts are up to you to guess. Needless to say, sometimes an image has to be flensed from the conscious mind. Writing can sometimes be the best therapy.

The Last Viewing

The Bijou Theater is a real place, a fact for which I am insanely happy. You can find it on the 101 in Lincoln City, Oregon, right near the middle of town. Last I heard, they were still doing a silent film night with an organist performing live. Go, enjoy, and step back in time for a couple of hours. While you're in Lincoln City, drop by McMenamins brew pub for dinner and a pint. Great stuff.

I spent two weeks in Lincoln City at a workshop run by a couple of wonderful professional writers who believe in paying it forward. They don't make enough money for the workshops for the time they take away from their own writing to make it financially prudent; they just can't give back to the people who gave to them early in their careers so, instead, they give what they know to those of us just starting out our professional careers. I'm still learning things about writing and about life from those two weeks, and the education I received from them will probably never end. So Kris, Dean, thank you.

One of the exercises at this workshop was to tour The Bijou, (with the kind permission of the management during off hours) and then to write a story overnight using the Bijou at the central location. "The Last Viewing," is the story I wrote between nine p.m. and two a.m. that night. Other than a few spelling corrections, the story in this collection appears exactly as written in that five hour span of time. If you're a writer and someone tells you that writing fast means writing poorly, tell them to go screw themselves. It just. Ain't. True.

You have my full permission to disagree. What works for me might not work for you, but you've got nothing to lose in the trying. When I stopped rewriting the life out of my fiction, the checks starting showing up in my mailbox. Your mileage may vary, of course, but don't count on it.

Copper Angels

This was a tuning fork story. The final image of this tale rattled around my head for close to ten years before I ever sat down to write it. I'm not sure why it took so long, but I'm glad it did. It's very possible that I wouldn't have been able to finish it otherwise. Some stories jump out and demand to be written. Some wait around and haunt you until your skills catch up to them.

Half the people who've read it seem to love it. The other half seem to hate it. When that happens, it usually means good things. Like the old saying goes, "You can't turn some people on without turning other people off." Don't be afraid to write what you want to write just because you feel it might offend someone. Thankfully Marti and Bridgett McKenna at Aeon magazine were in the camp that loved it.

Beyond that, affiant sayeth naught.

Malingering

Another workshop story, but instead of an assignment to write a complete tale, this started life as an exercise wherein a character had to carry on a conversation while performing a physical task with which the writer was familiar. I know very little about cars, but I do know about being short on cash so the one thing I learned was how to change the break pads on my old, used vehicles. When you're saving yourself over a hundred and fifty bucks by doing it yourself, you find the incentive to learn is a powerful one.

I had just overheard another writer discussing the concept of Peak Oil, and the two completely dissimilar ideas seemed like a good place to start. I was troubled by the dilemma the father and son faced enough to complete the story after the workshop. It was the first thing I wrote after getting home. I had to find out what happened to those three. Sometimes I still wonder what happens next. Maybe someday I'll find out and share it with you. Stranger things have happened.

Public Service

If you couldn't tell by now, that two week workshop I spoke about in Lincoln City, Oregon was intense. Public Service is another story assignment from that workshop. We were challenged to write a story set entirely in a public restroom.

Now I don't know about you, but I'm rather odd about having to use public restrooms. I'd rather not, to tell the truth, but if I just have to go number one, I don't think too much about it.

Anything more, however, makes me wince. It's stupid, but I never got over the tales about the germs and getting crabs and worst of all, the urban myth about the alligators in the sewers has stuck with me since I heard it. (I'm not alone in this respect; my ex-wife was terrified of something reaching up out of the toilet and grabbing her. I used to tape scary action figures across the bowl under the lid where'd she'd find them upon lifting the seat just to hear her scream. Did I mention she's my ex-wife?)

Throw in a dash of Raymond Chandler, add a sprig of H.P. Lovecraft, set it all in a public restroom and *viola!* One twisted little story.

Scratch

If you've read the story, (and if you haven't why are you reading this?), you know that, "Scratch," has absolutely, positively no socially redeeming qualities whatsoever. It's a story built to make you feel things crawling on your skin when you're done reading it, and to make you a little nervous the next time you have a genuine itch.

Some stories are born of ideas, some of inspiration and some of perspiration. This one was born of anger.

Back in 1995, I attended the Clarion West Science Fiction and Fantasy Writer's Workshop in Seattle. It's a six week live-in workshop and each week a new instructor arrived to act as writer-in-residence and teacher for that week. One of the teachers (And no, I will not name him) was a particular hero of mine. He was a World Fantasy Award winner, and one book in particular of his had been a personal favorite. I had a deep, important story I planned to write while he was there.

Yeah. Not so much.

The first day of teaching, he eviscerated a class-mate for writing a short, very amusing horror story. I believe the words he used in his critique were, "There's really no point in stories like this; beyond the momentary thrill."

After class I cornered him about his statement.

"Um, what about the ghost stories of Henry James?" I asked.

"That's different."

"No it's not. His stories were just as shocking for the mores of the time as any splatterpunk story written today."

He sniffed with his best Harvard-Professorial disinterest and said, "No. They're not."

"Okay," I said. "But you're wrong."

He walked off and I went back to my dorm room, opened up a new word file and wrote, "Scratch," in about two hours.

I really don't know what he thought of it. I didn't listen. All I know is that the story sold twice and made me an hourly wage of over four hundred bucks for the time I put into it.

The only reason I wrote this story was to say, "Screw you," to this guy, and you know what? I think I'll say it again:

Hey? Mr. Harvard creative writing type guy who wrote a book called something like, "Small, Huge? Go screw yourself.

Lesson to be learned? One should never confuse the art with the artist. The artist is usually so much less than the art. And never, ever mess with someone I care about. My classmate was at the time a beginning writer who wrote a good story and didn't deserve your scorn.

Oh yeah, one other lesson: Piss me off and I'll get even. It may take fifteen years, but it will happen.

Multiple Pages on a Monday Morning, From the Scrapbook of Infinite Possibilities

And yes, I'm well aware that this is one of the longest titles for a story ever.

Earlier I mentioned that I'd written two stories from a title alone. "Ten With a Flag," was the first. This is the second.

Samantha Henderson and I were at a convention (I believe it was NASFIC in Seattle) and the two of us had some time between our panels and panels we wanted to attend, so we decided to hit the art dealer's room.

Samantha and I loved to play little writing games with each other. At one point we created a string of flash fiction stories wherein the last word of one person's story had to be used for the start of the next person's story. One of those stories appears in this collection. But this time around we decided that we'd pick a piece of art from the art dealer's room and assign the other to write a story based upon that object/image. I can't remember what I assigned for her, but I remember her grabbing me by the shirt-sleeve and leading me to a small leather-bound book, encrusted with gaudy, fake jewels and banded with sturdy straps and buckles. In front of the book rested a placard that read, "The Book of Infinite Possibilities."

I did play football for a single year. I hated it. No, that's really not right. I loathed it with all my might. Worst part? I wasn't half bad. Realizing that I'd never written about it, and needing inspiration for the assigned story, it seemed like a good combination. Truth be told, this is probably my favorite story in the collection, and also the story that was most difficult to write. I hope you enjoyed it.

Ma, Gin and Bug-Eyed Aliens

Well, if you don't have a Redneck meets Aliens tale, you're not much of a writer are you? As you can tell from the story, this one was just a giggle to write and the quickest to sell of all my stories. I sent it off to the editor and within fifteen minutes had a reply in my inbox from the editor that said, "Okay. You got me. I actually laughed. Sold."

CC&R's at the Widdershins Parallelium

Once you start to publish stories, opportunities present themselves in odd places. One of the instructors at the Oregon Coast workshop contracted with Tekno Books to edit an anthology called, *Wizards, Inc.,* a collection of stories featuring people who made their living from magic. Loren had a couple spots left to fill so he put out a call for stories from the workshop attendees, due in three days. So I wrote this and had a blast doing it. It is a silly little story, and while I lost out by a hair to some very well known authors (Orson Scott Card has a story in the anthology, so I don't feel too bad), I figured I'd save it for my first collection instead of sending out such a specialized tale to the general market.

And if you get a chance, pick up *Wizards, Inc.* if you enjoy a little fantasy in your boardroom.

On the Nightside of the Ancient Walnut Moon

As anyone who's done it can tell you, growing into adulthood can be a bitch. When you're young, the last thing you want to do is commit to anything that will limit your options, or commit you for life. You're young, after all. You have your youth and the whole world is waiting for you to enjoy it and make your mark.

It's impossible to not go through a selfish phase, but we only learn later in life that choosing to be with the ones we love may be the most rewarding, selfish act there is.

For about a year, every dream I remembered upon waking took place in a single location. Yes, that's right. My subconscious mind created its own setting for my dreams, and over the course of that year I discovered and explored almost all of the town. The whorehouse without walls filled with chaste prostitutes, the castle on the hill, Johnny's Bar. . . and then one day the cycle of dreams ended for no seemingly good reason. In retrospect, the village of my dreams was nothing more than an amalgam of two places I knew well; Grantsville, West Virginia--my boyhood town--and *Bad Kreuznach,* a town in Germany just south of Mainz that I used to enjoy visiting. The combination of the ancient architecture of Germany and the abject poverty and natural beauty of West Virginia intrigued me and I knew I had to write a story set in this mash-up milieu. While the town ended up not being a large part of the story, it was nice to visit there again.

So, for your amusement, Peter Pan syndrome meets mystical village.

Pilgrimage

As I said earlier, stories come from everywhere. This particular piece of flash fiction came from a photograph I saw while surfing the net of an ancient stone wall somewhere in Ireland that immediately set me to wondering, *Why in the earth did they build that thing so tall? It's not like cows can jump* . . . As I was in a particularly grumpy mood that day, I wrote a few hundred words and shot it off to the editor of "Alien Skin," magazine. They bought it three days later. Not exactly a work of art, but writing it put me in a much better mood.

One great thing about writing? You get to vent your frustrations on imaginary people. As they say in New Orleans, the money from the sale is just *lagniappe.*

Menial Labor

I wrote this tale in the summer of 2005. I had just finished paying off my student loans from college at that point, and I was despairing for those who would follow me down the path of indentured servitude for the privilege of obtaining an education that could be used to obtain a livable wage. I won't go into my thoughts too deeply on this subject here, but there's something wrong with a system that requires you to spend the same amount of money you'd spend on a house just to obtain a piece of paper that makes you employable. There's too much knowledge available in this world for this system to be in place. Like someone once said, "In the United States, you've got to owe somebody to be somebody." It's a pity we feel the need to indoctrinate our children into the lifelong pursuit of debt at such a young age.

"Menial Labor," is a story I wrote to rail against the system of using someone's desire to better themselves for financial gain. I sent it out to a couple big name magazines without getting a bite, and soon after, Josh Whedon's *Dollhouse* premiered on television. So I retired the story, knowing that the comparisons and accusations of derivative work would soon follow.

It is appearing in print here for the first time.

And yes, it is a nasty little story. Watching people get screwed by a system that purports to help them will do that to me.

Reflections of a Similar Mind

Quantum physics has always fascinated me, while completely baffling me at the same time. One of the most famous quotes about this particular field comes from the American theoretical physicist, Richard Feyman, who said, "Anyone who says that they understand Quantum Mechanics does not understand Quantum Mechanics."

Well, he's half right. Those of us who admit to *not* understanding Quantum Mechanics also have no idea what we're talking about. I understand it just enough to get myself in trouble, but couldn't help but write this story anyway. That's the beauty of being a writer. When in doubt you can make up a pretty lie.

You walk a fine line when you write a story like this. While the doubtful side of you wants to explain everything in detail so you ensure the reader understands the story exactly as you intend, there's also the urge to treat your reader like an adult and let them work at it a little bit. You balance explaining too much with the need to throw the reader a bone every once in a while. I've gotten great feedback on this story and TQR Magazine picked it up and also published it in their, "Best of," anthology called, *Touching the Monkey,* so I can only assume that I didn't fall off the high-wire on this one.

Either way, I hope you enjoyed this story of Frankenstein in the quantum universe. And like the sage said, "The path to hell is paved with good intentions."

Or inventions, for that matter.

The Man Behind the Curtain

Losing a parent is the most difficult right of passage there is. Even when you didn't particularly care for that parent, they are the ones who brought you into the world and fed you and clothed you and bandaged your knee when you were learning to ride a bike and took you out for ice cream and hugged you in front of your friends.

When a parent you don't speak to dies, all the feelings of guilt come to the surface in a way that's unimaginable.

I wrote this story to deal with the death of my Mother, Sarah May Haines. Suzi is real, as are a number of parts of this story and the parts that are auto-biographical are probably not the parts you might think.

We all make mistakes. We're all stubborn in our own ways. Sometimes it takes magic to help you learn to forgive, and that magic can be as simple and all-powerful as the love of big sisters.

Conclusion

I hope you've enjoyed our little trip together. I know for certain that I did. There are simply too many people to thank for helping me along the way, but I'm going to try anyway.

All of the following people helped me or pushed me or gave me the strength to keep learning and keep writing:

Howard Waldrop, Joan Vinge, Michael Swanwick, Gardner Dozois, Katherine Dunn, Kristine Katherine Rusch, Dean Wesley Smith, Loren Coleman, my classmates from Clarion West 1995 and the Oregon Coast Professional Fiction Writer's Workshop Master's Class of 2003, Samantha Henderson, Lon Prater and the rest of the Critical MS critique group, Mark Hill for allowing me to use his incredible artwork for the book cover and last but certainly not least, to Harlan Ellison who made me realize that there might be a place for these crazy stories running around in my head. All of you have made my life better and the world a much more interesting place. Feeble as it is, all I have to offer you in return is my friendship and thanks.

If I forgot you, my apologies. The omission is my own.

Until next time,

Joseph Paul Haines
October, 2010

Joseph Paul Haines resides in Colorado with his wife, Catherine and his dog Buddy. He is currently at work on multiple stories and novels. You can find him online at www.josephpaulhaines.com